# HOLD A SCORPION

# HOLD
# A
# SCORPION

MELODIE JOHNSON HOWE

PEGASUS CRIME

NEW YORK LONDON

HOLD A SCORPION

Pegasus Books Ltd.
148 W 37th Street, 13th Floor
New York, NY 10018

First Pegasus Books cloth edition October 2016

Interior design by Maria Fernandez

Library of Congress Cataloging-in-Publication Data is available.

ISBN: 978-1-60598-967-9

10 9 8 7 6 5 4 3 2 1

Printed in the United States of America
Distributed by W. W. Norton & Company

*For Bones,*
*who brings love and music to my life.*
*The beat goes on.*

# HOLD A SCORPION

# CHAPTER ONE

I was bigger than life, running down the streets of Barcelona.

It was late afternoon and I sat in the dark watching myself on the big screen. The theater was sparsely attended, but that had nothing to do with the lack of an audience. The film was a flop. A turkey. A dud. It fit my mood.

Over lunch and too much wine, I had broken up with my lover. His wounded voice rattled in my head. He had told me that no man was ever going to live up to my expectations, that no man was ever going to please me, that I would end up old and alone, and I should take a good look at myself. So I did. I went to see a movie I was in.

Watching my image on the screen always splits me in two. The narcissistic side of me wallows in delight at my being loved by the camera. But narcissism is as demanding as an unpaid drug dealer. The other side of me, the sharp-as-an-axe critic, reminds me of the destructiveness of falling in love with my own image. I may look ten years younger but I was still forty-one—old by Hollywood standards. As my ex-lover warned, I could end up alone. And on top of all that, I was running to my death in a fiasco of a film.

Why I had to die was still as unclear as it was on the day I shot the scene. It was only obvious to Pedro Romero, the great Mexican director making his first American movie. An auteur of small influential films, he had been welcomed to Hollywood with a ton of money and an array of special effects. He, and therefore I and the other actors, had drowned in Hollywood's largesse and Romero's ego. The only stars left standing were the special effects guys, which meant the movie was big in China because they loved special effects. But it was still a flop in America.

I, who usually kept my hope in check, had had such faith in this movie. I thought it would secure me larger roles and more money. I had fallen into the Hollywood trap of this-is-my-big-chance syndrome. I knew better. You just take the parts as they come, and you go on.

Closing my eyes against my fleeing image, against the memory of my ex-lover's stiffening jaw and hurt eyes, I fell asleep. When I awoke with a start, feeling slightly hungover, the theater was empty and the movie had begun again. It hadn't gotten any better.

But I should have stayed to watch it one more time.

# CHAPTER TWO

The sun was balancing on the rim of the ocean, its light slanting into the driver's side window of my old green Jag, warming my left cheek. Traffic was heavy as I headed to my home on PCH—Pacific Coast Highway—in Malibu. Surfers, finished for the day, were strapping their boards on the top of their cars parked along the side of the road. Some had unzipped their wet suits down to their narrow pale hips then wrapped long towels like sarongs around their waists. Now they were adeptly slipping their wet suits off beneath their chaste covering. In all my years of living in Malibu I had never seen one towel fall. But there is always hope. In an ode to bad taste, the American Apparel building rose up, jarringly out of place with its baby blue–tinted windows reflecting

its big asphalt parking lot, draped with a banner that declared: OUR
CLOTHES ARE MADE IN DOWNTOWN LOS ANGELES. Hollywood isn't the only
business that thrives on hype.

Now the ocean disappeared from sight and all there was to see
were homes lining the coast. Jammed together and vying for space,
they cut off any view of the Pacific. Mine was among them.

As I drove into my carport, Ryan Johns was waiting for me with
a bouquet of flowers.

"I need to talk with you." He pulled open the car door.

"You brought me flowers?"

"No. Did you break up with the Ego?" That's what he called my
now ex-lover, Peter Bianchi.

"I did."

"About time. I think they're from him."

"You read the card?"

"I got bored waiting." He was wearing his usual outfit: Hawaiian
shirt, baggy Bermuda shorts, and Uggs.

"Did he leave them?" I didn't like the idea of Peter Bianchi
driving to my house after we broke up.

"I don't know. I've had a revelation." Ryan was bouncing nervously on the balls of his feet.

I opened the card. It read: *You'll be sorry, Diana. You'll never find a*
*man as right for you as I am.* I sighed. I didn't want a man who knew
he was "right" for me.

"Diana, did you hear what I said? This is important." Ryan
moved in front of me. His red hair sprouted wildly from his head,
his intense blue eyes, not yet blurred from alcohol, fixed on mine.

"You had a revelation. You're a writer. That's what you get paid
for."

"But I've never had one I didn't know what to do with. What good
is an epiphany if you don't know what to do with it?"

"Then it's not one." I paused, taking in his anxious expression.
"What is it, Ryan?"

"I'm in the twilight of a bullshit career." He spoke as if it hurt him physically to say the words.

I put my hand on his arm. "No, you're not."

"I'm writing a movie about zombies, for fuck's sake!"

"Zombies are hot."

"Zombies are over, Diana. Every simile, metaphor, and analogy has been drained out of them along with their lives and blood. I'm on the tail end of a trend. I was always ahead of the curve. The first to sense a new thing."

Glancing over his shoulder, I saw a woman flapping her hands in the air. Across the four-lane highway, she stood on the dirt embankment in the shadow of the mountain that jutted up, towering above PCH and our houses.

"What's that woman doing?" I asked.

Following my gaze, he turned. "Looks like she's waving at you. Do you know her?"

"No, I don't think so." Still holding my flowers, I walked down to the apron of my short drive to get a better view of her. Cars sped by, heading south toward Sunset Boulevard or Santa Monica. The woman was maybe in her sixties, with long dark brown hair and fair, glistening skin that appeared flushed, as if she'd been walking fast or running. Her heavy body was covered with a long blue caftan. Gesturing, she smiled at me, or at least in my direction.

"Maybe she's a fan," Ryan said, standing behind me now.

"Maybe she's waving at you?"

"Screenwriters don't have fans who wave madly at us."

A few yards from the woman a black SUV pulled off the highway and came to a stop on the embankment. The passenger-side door opened. The woman looked at it, and then at the oncoming traffic, as if she saw what we all saw—automobiles rushing by her at speeds from fifty to eighty miles an hour. Then she gazed back at me and walked, smiling, into the onslaught of cars.

A white van rammed full force into her, flipping her into the air, hair splintered out from her head. In the next lane, a beige sedan ran over her as she hit the pavement. The van and sedan slammed on their brakes and stopped. Horns blared. The cars behind them skidded and screeched, trying not to rear-end or sideswipe each other. Bumpers smashed. Taillights cracked.

"Oh, my God." Dropping the flowers, I dug my cell phone out of my purse and called 911. Then I ran back to my car and grabbed a blanket from the trunk.

Ryan loped toward his house, which was next to mine, yelling, "Shit, shit, shit!"

The northbound lanes had come to a complete stop. Going south had now slowed to a crawl. I darted between the inching cars to where the woman lay. An elderly couple, ashen and confused, got out of the beige sedan and crept toward the back of it to see what lay there.

In the lane next to them the driver of the van walked in a circle hitting the sides of his head with his hands, groaning, "I didn't see her, I didn't see her."

Behind the sedan a teenage girl leaped out of her Subaru. Another man, sweat running down the sides of his face, breathing hard, kneeled next to the woman. Her face was as gray as the asphalt. Brown eyebrows, arched over eyes that stared blankly at the darkening sky. Blood oozed from the back of her head mixing with her dyed brown hair. Her blue caftan had bunched up, revealing large dimpled thighs and a belly encased in slimming Spanx underwear. The man gently pulled at the hem of the caftan so that it covered her knees. He lifted his head, looking at me.

Touched by his gallant gesture, I said, "That was kind."

"She was running to you," he said.

Before I could respond, the teenager blurted, "*They* ran over her, not me!" She pointed at the elderly couple that was also peering down at the dead woman.

"I couldn't stop, I couldn't stop." The old man's hands shook.

"She seemed to fall from the sky." His wife looked up as if to discover what had dropped the woman down in front of their car.

I stood up and wrapped the blanket around her trembling shoulders.

Ryan appeared with a pile of brightly striped beach towels emblazoned with images of topless hula dancers. He draped one around the bewildered man's stooped shoulders. He offered one to the teenager, who turned away from him as she took her cell phone from her pocket. Then he went over to the driver of the van and put one around his shoulders.

"She was just there in front me. Just there, in front me," the man repeated, twisting the corner of the towel in his hands.

Some drivers were now out of their cars talking on their cells, surveying the damage to their vehicles. The teenager sobbed into her phone. I heard the word *mom*.

PCH was at a dead stop going both ways. Wisps of fog began to wave in from the ocean and curl around us. The sun had disappeared leaving us in a dusky gray-lavender light. The sound of police sirens and ambulances cut through the chaos. The loud, agitated horns of the fire trucks blared, forcing autos out of their way.

Two motorcycle cops made their way between the unmoving cars and came to a stop near us. Getting off his bike, one squatted down and checked the woman. The other began directing traffic to make way for the emergency vehicles.

I noticed the man who had pulled down the dead woman's dress had disappeared. Standing on my tiptoes, I searched over the mass of jammed cars, but I couldn't see him. Automobiles were now edging onto the dirt side of the highway, trying to maneuver around the accident and get on with their lives. The black SUV that I had seen stop was gone.

The motorcycle cop stood up. "Who saw what happened?"

I described what I'd seen. When I finished, the cop strode over to the driver of the van.

The teenager followed the cop, her phone still to her ear. "I saw it all. The woman was running towards her." She pointed back at me. "She was holding flowers," she added as if that was the reason for the accident that had brought all of their lives to a sudden, terrible halt.

Coming into view, patrol cars and emergency vehicles, their lights swirling and mixing with the thickening fog, worked their way toward us.

I stared back down at the dead body. The bigger-than-life me who had rejected a lover and fallen asleep watching the camera love me had vanished. A woman had just been obliterated from this earth. And it made me feel insignificant and vulnerable.

I didn't realize I was shivering until Ryan draped one of his beach towels over my shoulders.

# CHAPTER THREE

We all fear oblivion, but Hollywood fears it more. In show business you can still be alive but not exist. You wake up one morning and your name is meaningless. Your face and your talent no longer command attention. You might as well be dead. But it's worse because you're not.

The death of the woman last night had stirred that fear in Ryan, which had already been growing inside of him before the accident. He had gotten drunk and passed out. I had gone to bed with a new script, clinging to it as if it were a piece of wreckage that would save me from the nothingness.

I was up for a nice-size role as the love interest in a film starring Luke Able. He was in his late fifties and still able to open a movie.

But I couldn't concentrate. I kept thinking of the man who had pulled the woman's caftan down, of his words: "She was running to you." Were his eyes filled with accusation? Hers were empty.

I turned on the TCM channel, took two sleeping pills, and fell asleep with the script spread across my breasts. I died in this movie too.

The next morning the fog had rolled in. June Gloom. The one month of summer where the beach is shrouded in a heavy gray mist and the tourists shiver in their new swimsuits. I paced my small wooden deck, an old wide-brimmed straw hat shoved down on my head, a cup of coffee in one hand, and the script in the other. I read my lines out loud, letting the breeze carry them off toward the ocean. "You don't think I could kill her, do you?" I demanded from a seagull that had just alighted on the railing. He eyed me like a director who didn't want to hire me. "Well, do you?" I ad-libbed, then swatted the bird away with the script.

Begrudgingly, he flew off but not before he left me a dollop of poop.

A loud snort interrupted what was left of my concentration, and I glanced toward Ryan's house. It towered above my small 1970s bungalow—one of the few remaining homes that had not been remodeled. Still in his clothes from yesterday, Ryan was asleep, spread-eagled, on one of his many lounges that lined his long verandah. His house looked like an expensive boutique hotel, its empty chaises facing the Pacific, waiting for guests who would never arrive.

"Ryan, wake up. You're going to get sunburned," I yelled at him across our common pathway.

He kicked his legs; one of his Uggs fell off. His bare foot was as pale as a sun-bleached bone. My cell phone rang. I picked it up from the umbrella table and saw Peter Bianchi's name. Hell.

"Hi, Peter," I said in a neutral voice.

"Are you all right? A friend of mine told me there was a terrible accident in front of your house. A woman died. I just wanted to make sure that it . . ."

"Wasn't me?"

"Yes."

"Well, it wasn't."

"How are you?" His voice lowered, more intimate.

"Peter . . ."

"Did you get my flowers?"

I could feel the ribbon-bound bouquet sliding from my hands when the woman was struck by the van. I shivered. "Did you bring them to my house?"

"Yes. I thought you might be there."

"I went to the movies. I have to go. I have an interview this afternoon and I'm way behind . . ."

"I just wanted you to know that I'm not going to tweet about our breakup."

"Tweet? What are we, teenagers?"

"We were what they call an item, Diana. You got a lot of free publicity being with me. I could almost think you used me for that."

"I don't know if you're capable of hearing what you just said, Peter, but that is an example of why we're not together anymore."

Did he always act this way? Childish? Covering his own ass? No, not his ass, his image. Christ, what did that say about me?

"Well, be careful. Obviously, anything can happen," he added.

"What do you mean by that?" There was no answer. He had already disconnected.

Disturbed, I walked into my living room and threw my script onto the sofa. I shouldn't have broken my rule to never get involved with an actor. We had met on the Romero film while we were on location in Barcelona. That was another rule I broke. End the affair when the making of the movie ends. Never, never, try to drag it back into reality because it was never real to begin with. Actually that was Nora's, my movie star mother's, rule.

I looked at my empty fireplace mantel. I had swept it clean by taking my mother's urn, still filled with her ashes, and my husband's Oscars and any other photographs of him and put them all in his office, off the kitchen. Colin had died from a heart attack two years ago. Was it only two years? And I still felt that deep loss, except now it was numbed around its sharp edges with the knowledge that even a man who loves you can betray you. And so can your mother. Another rule broken: Don't try to hide your ghosts in a room off the kitchen. It doesn't work.

I picked up a puffy hydrangea in a plastic pot from the coffee table and placed it in the center of the mantel, stepped back, and surveyed my work. Pathetic.

When performing on stage, an actor needs to create a sense of place. She must turn a piece of bosom wood furniture, a fake wall, or a door that leads nowhere, and make it real. Bette Davis went so far as to say that she didn't just sit on a sofa, she made love to it. The actor owns nothing except her entrance. Her job is to make the audience believe that just by walking onstage she is entering a room so familiar that they know in their hearts that she was loved there and hurt there.

I was trying to create a sense of place in my own home, in real life as they say. One of the great things about Hollywood is you can make money while failing. With the money I'd earned from the flop, I had fixed my rotting wood deck and replaced the sliding doors with French ones. I even tried to have the heater on my Jag fixed, but it still had a personality of its own. At least the locks worked now.

I moved the potted plant to the end of the mantel, thinking if it were off-center it wouldn't look so desperate. The doorbell rang.

Letting out a sigh, I went to the foyer and peered out the peephole. I saw a sheriff's badge sagging from the breast pocket of a khaki shirt, and above the buttoned-up collar a glimpse of a double chin. I opened the door.

"Ms. Poole? I'm Deputy Sheriff Ford, Malibu Sheriff Station. It's so nice to meet you. I'm a fan of yours." He stuck his hand out. I shook it, returning his strong grip. "I'm here to ask you a few questions about the accident that you witnessed last night."

Christ, if my day kept on this way I wasn't going to have a chance in hell of dying in Luke Able's movie.

# CHAPTER FOUR

Deputy Sheriff Ford stood in the living room near the fireplace. He was a big man with a broad chest and long thin legs. His shape reminded me of an upside-down bowling pin. Thick white hair showed off his tan, weathered face, which almost gave him character. But not quite. His hazel eyes were too careful. His nose too turned up. Too cute. I judged him to be in his mid fifties, maybe an ex-surfer, probably an ex–frat boy. He had declined to sit down.

I swept my straw hat off my head, fluffed my determinedly blond hair, and sat on the sofa. "I don't have much time. I have to be at Warner Bros."

"What movie are you shooting?"

"I'm reading for a part."

"Well, I hope you get it. You were the best thing in Romero's film."

"You saw it?"

"I like to see the work of the many creative people who live in our community." His words sounded prepared, as if he were talking to reporters.

He took out a small tape recorder and hit a button. I heard voices being rewound, sounding like geese at a cocktail party. He hit two more buttons and held it to his ear, nodding to something he heard. "I'm going to be recording our conversation. Do you mind?"

"It was just an accident, wasn't it?"

"Yes, it was. I but I like to cross all my *t*'s and dot my *i*'s."

Agreeing, I could feel myself tense. He sat his sleek little recorder on the coffee table and said, "A few witnesses seem to think or imply that you might know the dead woman?"

"I didn't know her."

"But she was waving at you?"

"She was waving. I'm not sure it was at me. I even walked down to the end of my driveway to get a better look at her, to see if I recognized her."

"And you didn't?"

I nodded, then remembered he was recording me. "No, I did not."

"How about this screenwriter you were with . . ." He took a notepad out of his pant pocket and flipped through it. "Ryan Johns."

"He didn't know her either."

"I rang his doorbell. Nobody answered."

I thought of Ryan spread-eagled on his chaise lounge. "He's out."

He shifted his weight. "You had some flowers in your hand?"

"Yes, but not for the woman. I mean they had nothing to do with the accident. There was a man kneeling next to her. Maybe he knew her. He left before the police came."

His careful eyes grew sharp. "What did he look like?"

"He had small hands. I remember them because of his gallant gesture."

"What kind of gesture?"

"*Gallant.* He pulled the hem of her dress down." The accident was coming back to me full force, jarring me, pushing me off-center like the stupid hydrangea plant on the mantel.

"Anything else?"

"Brownish hair neatly combed. That's about it."

"Height?"

"He was kneeling. But I had the feeling he wasn't very tall. But there's no way I can be sure."

"Did the two of you talk?"

I let out a long breath. "He said she, meaning the woman, was running to me."

He raised his eyebrows.

"Look, I'm an actress," I went on as if I had to justify myself. "Maybe she thought she knew me. But she didn't. It happens."

He sucked in his belly and glanced around the room. I sensed he was slightly disappointed with my slapdash décor. "Anything else you can remember?"

"She was wearing Spanx under an expensive looking caftan."

"Spanx?"

"Underwear that slims you."

"Okay."

"I mean it's odd. Most women don't wear Spanx under a loose-fitting caftan."

"I'll remember that." He reached for his recorder, clicked it off, and slipped it back into his pocket. "Thank you for your help, Ms. Poole." He started for the front door.

"There is another possibility," I said.

"What's that?" He swung around, facing me.

"Maybe the woman wasn't running *to* something but *from* something." I already regretted my words. It was his accident to figure out, not mine.

"What makes you think that?"

"The man was sweating."

"What man?"

"The one who pulled her dress down."

"The *gallant* one."

"Yes. And right before she ran into the traffic, an SUV pulled off on the side of the highway. I think someone got out of it. But I didn't see who it was."

"Can you describe the vehicle?"

"It was a dark color, probably black. Maybe a Range Rover."

"You've thought a lot about this."

"I keep running the accident over and over in my head. It's not an easy thing to forget."

"No, it's not. Sorry to bring it all up again. Well, good luck with your interview."

I opened the front door for him. He walked outside and stopped, looking back at me. "You would tell me if you knew her, right? I mean, you have no reason not to tell me," he said, his tired eyes on me. The morning sun danced on his thick head of hair. He had once been a handsome man before something or someone had worn him down.

"I told you, I've never seen her before. I hope you find out who she is."

"Oh, we've already identified her." He turned and began to walk away.

I shut the door.

Not moving, I stood in my dimly lit foyer, feeling as if I had been accused of something, as if I were a suspect. But of what? And why so many questions about a woman they'd already identified?

I walked back into the living room just in time to see Ryan sway up on my deck, lean over the railing, and puke.

# CHAPTER FIVE

D amn it, Ryan. Couldn't you have done that off your own balcony?"

He wiped his mouth with the back of his freckled hand, blinking his golden-red eyelashes. "Sorry."

The creases and wrinkles in his Hawaiian shirt had bent the beckoning hula dancers out of shape, making them look grotesque. Behind him, the ocean rolled and crashed. Sandpipers paced.

"I'll have my guy clean it up with a power hose."

"You don't have a guy."

"My gardener. You know I dreamed about her," he added softly.

"The dead woman?"

He nodded. "I never dream when I'm passed out. I mean that's the point of drinking yourself into a stupor, isn't it?"

"Come in and have a cup of coffee and help me with my lines. I have an interview later."

"I'd prefer vodka. Take the edge off?" He tried to look innocent.

"Coffee."

"Beer?"

"Then get it at your own house."

"Tough love. But it's love." He wiggled his eyebrows at me then winced with the effort.

In the kitchen, I poured him coffee and told him about my conversation with Deputy Sheriff Ford.

"So they identified her, " he said."What's her name?"

"He didn't tell me."

"I'd like to know her name."

"Why would a woman wear Spanx under a caftan?"

"Uh? What's that?"

Christ. "It's a contemporary version of a girdle. Don't you men ever have to struggle with women's underwear when you're trying to get them into bed?"

"Not really. I mean a thong is pretty much as difficult as it gets."

"The point is, a woman puts a loose dress like that on so she doesn't have to wear anything that binds her or that feels tight around her."

His blurry blue eyes widened. "Really? You mean they don't have anything on under those caftans?"

"Oh God, you'd turn anything into a sexual fantasy." I paused. "Peter Bianchi called me," I said, changing the subject. "He said he wouldn't tweet about us breaking up." I felt foolish even saying it.

"He will."

"Why did I get involved with him?"

"Rebound," Ryan said.

"What?"

"You never would've gotten involved with him if it hadn't been for Leo Heath."

"This has nothing to do with Heath." I remembered Heath cupping my cheek with his hand, asking me if I would ever want to see him again. But before I could answer, he had walked away. It was the last time I saw him. Why hadn't he waited for my answer?

"Diana, all I know is," Ryan said, "that when you didn't see Heath anymore you got stupid."

"I never get stupid."

"Then how do you account for having an affair with an asshole? A triple asshole. But what do I know? I'm haunted by a dead woman, and I'm at the end of my career."

"Stop saying that. Bring your coffee into the living room."

I sat on the sofa and picked up the script. Ryan put his coffee on the table then walked over to the fireplace mantel, surveying it. "I miss Colin's Oscars, I even miss you mother's urn. Maybe it was lucky for Colin that he died before his writing career did."

"He wasn't lucky, Ryan. And your career isn't ending."

"Zombies are over and nobody knows it but me. It's not easy being the only one who knows the truth, who knows what's really trending." He moved the hydrangea back to the center of the mantel. "That's better than staring at nothing." He faced me. "I think you need to let your mother go."

"Where did that come from?"

"You still have her ashes. You should scatter them."

I tossed him the script and he caught it. "You play Charlie, Luke Able's role," I told him.

"He's over too, he just doesn't know it."

"Ryan, stop it. Some of us are still working on a little hope here."

"Sorry. I can't help it." He slumped down across from me in a new linen slipcovered chair I had just bought. A chair I had yet to sit in. I don't do well with change.

"Seeing that woman get hit . . . " He rubbed his forehead. " It just made everything seem meaningless. Maybe that's why I'm thinking of your mother. You have to honor the dead, Diana. Let's scatter her ashes now."

"No!" I wasn't ready to let go of the little I had of her, which was never very much. She had died alone at the Bel Air Hotel. A bottle of bourbon on the nightstand and an empty shot glass in her hand.

"Just trying to help." He peered at the script and began to read from it. "'Mark, you know me.'"

"That's my line."

"Sorry. 'I know you killed her,'" he mumbled.

"'Mark, you know me. How could you think I would kill her?'" I leaned toward Ryan. "'You've made love to me.'"

"'You killed her,'" he read flatly and yawned. "God, this is bullshit writing. It's all bullshit."

"Ryan, you're not helping me."

"Sorry. 'I'll find a way to prove you did it.'"

I stood, walking toward my French doors repeating the stage directions. "Now I put my arms around Luke Able and try to kiss him. He holds me at arm's distance, and I say, 'No, you won't.'" I whirled around facing Ryan. "'You love me, Mark, you love me.'"

Sound asleep, Ryan's head lolled back, his eyes closed, mouth open, and legs akimbo. The script dangled from his hand. I gently took it from him and went to get ready for the interview.

In my bedroom, I decided that the conflicted Luke Able would fall for a woman who dressed simply. So I put on jeans, a simple white silk shirt with the sleeves rolled up, and suede driving shoes. Back in the living room, I left the snoring Ryan a note that told him to lock up before he left and to clean up his puke. As I propped the note against the potted plant on the mantel he leaped straight up out of his chair yelling, "Get away from me! Get away!"

I jumped. "Ryan! You scared the hell out of me."

He looked wildly around the room. "She was here, right here standing in front of me, looking at me, searching my face for . . . what?" He clamped his hands on his head, tamping down his wild curls.

"Who was?"

"*The woman.*"

"You had a bad dream."

"She was in this room, Diana."

"She's dead, Ryan. You're hallucinating. It's the booze."

"No, she's haunting me. They haunt you when they're not dead. Or not dead enough."

"You told me zombies were over."

"In the movies."

"Ryan, your unconscious is mixing up your script with the accident. You're still drunk. Go home, go to bed."

"She'll come back to me if I sleep."

"I gotta go." I grabbed the script and my purse, then stopped. "Ryan, are you okay? I mean *really* okay?"

"I have to fix this." He was already slouching out onto the deck. I stared at the potted plant. It wasn't better than nothing. I put it back on the coffee table.

# CHAPTER SIX

T he Warner Bros. sound stages were hunkered down on Barham Boulevard in Burbank. On thick stucco walls hung giant billboards touting the studio's latest movies and TV shows.

Corporate high-rise buildings rose up through the smog, dwarfing the famous water tank with its Warner Bros. logo. Only in Southern California where water had always been fought over could a rickety, now empty tank be a legendary Hollywood landmark.

Luke Able's office was in one of the old 1920s Spanish-style buildings surrounding a quadrangle of cool dark green grass. I have always thought of this quad as the heart of the studio. But the tall office buildings housing hundreds of lawyers, too many executives, assistants, accountants, yes-men, and yes-women pressed in on this small area of the past. A past that once had more future than the movies did now.

Luke Able was taller on screen that he was in person. And I was glad I wore my loafers. His light brown shifty eyes and his manic style of acting had carried him through many starring roles.

Now, after all the *hellos* and *you-look-greats* we stood face-to-face, each holding a script. The producer was secured behind his desk. The director sat near him, legs extended, hands clasped behind his head as if he were sitting by a pool waiting for his margarita.

"Let's take this nice and easy," he said. "Anytime you're ready, Diana."

I focused on Luke's face and heard my voice say my first line, firm and strong even though my heart was fluttering. As the scene progressed I forgot about my nervousness. I threw my arms around Luke Able's broad shoulders. His breath smelled like a deli. He didn't push me away as it said in the script. He was giving only half of a performance, no sign of the manic energy the audience loved. I slowly withdrew my embrace as if realizing my lies were no longer working. I even managed to squeeze out one tear from my right eye, letting it roll down my check. I don't know where it had come from. I'm not one of those actresses who can cry on cue, but I hoped the producer and director saw it.

They did. The producer leaped to his feet. "Brava, Diana!"

The director leaned forward, resting his arms on his knees, and said, "You're better than your mother, Diana." There was the comparison again. But I humbly demurred, though I didn't feel humble.

"But how was I?" Luke asked, aiming for humor but sounding desperate.

We all laughed and told him how great he was.

When I left the office, I knew I had aced the role. I also knew not to think I had it. I'd been through too many interviews where I'd given great readings and didn't get the part. In other professions, you do a great job and usually get something back; the surgeon heals the patient, the salesman gets a trip to Miami because he was a top seller. Yet an actor can act her soul out and end up with just a lot of air-kisses.

Walking downstairs, I was still feeling the warmth of success when I saw her coming into the building. Gabrielle Hays. She paused for a moment to take off her sunglasses. Blond hair lush around her face, her features were broader than mine, giving a rough edge to her beauty. I stopped. She looked up and saw me, a wry smile forming on her sharp lips as she approached. Dark circles had formed under her eyes. Alas, they didn't make her appear tired. Instead they gave her a ravished decadent look.

"Let me guess, the Luke Able movie." Her voice was low, softer than her looks. "It always seems to come down to the two us, Diana."

After they weeded the field of other forty-something actresses, I thought.

"I heard there was a terrible accident near your house," she added.

"Yes." Car crashes on PCH were always news for some reason.

"You saw it happen?" She tossed her head like a beautiful thoroughbred.

"It was awful."

"Grist for the creative mill."

"I suppose you could look at it that way. Well, good luck," I said.

She moved past me on the stairs. Our shoulders bumped. She didn't wish me luck.

I hated Gabrielle Hays. I had tried not to, but slowly I had just given in to it. She was my doppelgänger. My evil twin. My nemesis. A blond shadow competing with my own blond shadow. In seconds, I had plunged from confidence to insecurity, and I hadn't even gotten down the damn stairs.

Outside, I slapped on my sunglasses and wondered whether I got under Gabrielle's skin the way she did mine. Heading around the corner of the building, I saw Peter Bianchi walking toward me.

"Diana!"

Stiffening, I asked, "What are you doing here?"

"Working."

Then I noticed the Kleenex stuffed around the collar of his gray shirt to prevent his makeup from rubbing off on it. Dark stubble still showed under his thick beige layering.

"Think I was following you?" His eyes shined like patent leather over a curved nose and full lips.

"Yes, I did."

Letting out a sigh, he shook his head, and a strand of his black hair flopped on his forehead. "I'm not a stalker."

"You threatened me this morning."

"No, I didn't. I was worried about you. What are you up for?"

"Luke Able's movie."

" Luke's a great guy. I'll put in a good word for you."

"Peter, don't. Please."

As I started to leave, he took my elbow, stopping me. "I miss you."

"I have a long drive back to Malibu."

"I think you should know that I did tweet about our breakup."

I thought of Ryan telling me Peter would. "You said you weren't going to."

"I had to tell my fans."

"Fine."

"I told them that I broke up with you. You're not going to contest that, right?"

"Peter, we're not in court. We're two adults who had an affair, and now it's over. What does it matter how it ended? And why does it have to be made public?"

"Because the public will want to know, at least about me. *Inside Edition* and TMZ probably have it by now. I just wanted to give you a heads-up in case you're asked."

How could I have not seen the depth of his shallowness? It had swallowed up his humor, stripped him of his charming self-deprecation. Where did his seductive personality go? Or did my rejection of him bring out his true petty self? "What exactly did you say? In case I'm asked."

"That due to the ten years difference in our ages, I wasn't ready to settle down."

"What? You implied that I wanted to get married to you because I'm old?"

"I didn't say anything about marriage. It could have just been us living together."

"I was the one who didn't want to move in with you. You make me sound like some cloying, desperate aging woman. A cougar with matted hair."

Applause wafted from an open window. I turned toward the warm, loving sound coming from the same corner room where I had done my reading. They were applauding Gabrielle Hays. Not moving, I felt trapped between the seductive sound of applause and the un-seductive Peter Bianchi and thought this must be what purgatory is like. Then I whirled around to Peter. "Take your tweet and shove it up your ass."

It was a slow grind back to Malibu. Traffic was at a standstill. And so was I emotionally. Jammed. Tight. I wasn't mad at Peter. He was being true to himself. It was me. I was the one who knew I was making a mistake. And then there was the sound of that applause. I could see Gabrielle basking in it. Behind me the guy laid on his car horn. Startled, I realized the traffic had begun to move and I was still at a standstill.

Edging forward, I peered into the rearview mirror, eyeing the man in his car. "Do you know who I am?" I demanded. "I'm Diana Poole. Unable to keep my hands off young men, unable to garner applause for my reading. Unable to scatter my mother's ashes."

My cell rang again. I grabbed it, thinking it was my agent. Hope and doom shot through me at the same time. I hit my brakes, almost crashing into the car in front of me. The man behind me slammed on his, leaning on his horn again.

"Is this Diana Poole?" an unfamiliar voice asked. For a crazy moment I thought it was the driver of the car in back of me.

"Who is this?" I asked.

"I was at the accident. I need to talk to you about the dead woman. Can we meet somewhere?"

"I think if you have any information you should talk to the sheriff's department."

"No. I need to talk to you. It's very important."

"This is a private number. How did you get it?"

"No number is private. Please, I need to talk to you about Elizabeth."

"Is that the dead woman?"

Silence.

"What's your name?"

"I can't give it to you."

"Are you the man who pulled her dress down?"

"We need to talk. Please, it's very important."

"Look, I'm sorry, but I can't help you. Call Deputy Sheriff Ford." I hung up.

I inched the Jag forward. The guy behind me was right on my tail, crowding me. The phone call had unnerved me. I didn't know any Elizabeth. I didn't know anything. But the caller thought I did. Ford thought I did. Way down deep, I knew my world was beginning to go in a direction I didn't want it to.

# CHAPTER SEVEN

t was 6:30 when I finally drove into my carport. Turning off the ignition, I leaned my head against the steering wheel. I was hungry, I needed a drink, and I felt alone. I lifted my head and froze.

In the dim light, a man stood in front of the Jag. Shadows carved deep holes under his eyes and down the sides of his mouth. He moved quickly around to my side of the car, motioning for me to get out. I recognized his hands first: small, plump, and shaking, as they were the night of the accident when he kneeled by the woman. Heart pounding, I pressed the door locks down. Nothing happened. Shit, you can never depend on a Jag.

"I just want to talk to you about the dead woman," he shouted through the car window.

"I told you, call Sheriff Ford." I fumbled with my keys, yelling back.

"I knew you were going to be difficult." He pulled a gun from his leather jacket. "Get out of the car." He tried to sound tough but his voice ended in a whine. The pistol jerked around in his trembling hands, making me even more frightened.

"I don't know anything about her." Shaking, I managed to insert the key in the ignition and throw the car in reverse. I shot backward and had to brake hard before I crashed into the speeding traffic. Oh, hell. There were no quick getaways in Malibu.

The man was at my window again, banging the flat side of his gun against it as he tried to pull the car door open. Holding onto the handle with one hand, I slammed the other on the horn, holding it down. At the sound of the blaring noise, he stashed the gun back in his jacket, and beat it down the side of the highway, disappearing into the darkness.

Heart leaping against the wall of my chest, I released my hand and the honking stopped. Nobody came out to see what was going on. Most homes along the coast, including Ryan's, were sound-proofed. Besides, what's another bleating car horn in Southern California? At least it scared him off.

Putting the car in drive, I rolled into the carport again and sat staring at the blank wall trying to gather myself. I grabbed my cell and called the Malibu sheriff's station. Deputy Sheriff Ford was out but I was told he would return my call as soon as possible.

Slinging my purse over my shoulder, I got out of the car. My eyes searched for any shadow that moved. Running up my walkway to the front door, I stopped dead. He was there, waiting for me.

He shoved his arms out, palms facing me, as if to tell me he wasn't dangerous. "I know you don't know anything about Eliza-beth. Here." He pulled the gun from his jacket.

Breathing hard, I stumbled backward.

"Take it." He thrust the butt of it toward me. "It has the safety catch on. I never intended to hurt you."

"I don't want your gun. I want you to leave."

"I could be in danger," he gasped.

"I'm in danger from you."

He laid the pistol on the ground between us. "See? I don't want to hurt you. I just want the scorpion."

"I don't know what you're talking about."

"She had it. They had her on pills." He spoke rapidly, running his words together. "But she didn't know you. But did. Or you were some other woman."

My head was pounding. "Stop talking!" I screamed at him.

He clamped his cupid lips shut. We stood in silence. My heart was thudding around again. I took a deep breath and looked at my small house, its dusty porch light shedding yellow on the potted geraniums that needed watering and this short baby-faced man, with baby-plump hands, and big frantic eyes, wearing a leather jacket he wasn't tough enough for.

And then I heard myself say, "I read for a part today in a Luke Able movie."

"Cool."

So this is what my life had come to—sharing news with a distraught crazy man. Yet it seemed to relax him a little.

"I hope you get it," he added.

"Thank you. Who are *'they'*?"

"Uh?"

"The people who had her on pills."

"I can't tell you."

That did it. I'd had enough. I took a deep breath. "Step aside," I ordered him in the cop voice I'd once used as a guest star in an episode of *Castle*. Obeying, he moved away from the door. I strode to it, unlocked it, ducked inside, slammed it shut, and slid the dead bolt into place. He pounded on it, pleading with me to talk to him.

"I'm calling 911 right now," I shouted through the door.

He stopped banging. I waited, leaning against the wall.

"You'll be sorry," he said, then there was silence.

After a few moments, I peered out the peephole. He was gone. Or least I couldn't see him.

I went around the house, turning on all the lights and making sure every door and window was locked. After pouring myself a large glass of red wine, I went into the living room and stared at my new linen-covered chair. Sitting down in it for the first time, I looked at the room from an unfamiliar perspective. I liked the newness of the view. It felt like I had moved to another house that didn't have ghosts and a crazy man waving a gun at me. Taking another gulp, I remembered that he was the second man today who had told me that I was going to be sorry. What was it that women had to be sorry for? Or that I in particular had to be sorry for? Witnessing a terrible accident that I couldn't have prevented? Ending an affair? Okay, I could have prevented the affair. *You'll be sorry.* That was a threat disguised as a warning. And who was Elizabeth? What kind of scorpion did he think I had? A live one? Dead one? And who were *they*? I gulped more wine.

My cell rang. Thinking it was Ford calling me back, I grabbed it.

"Diana Poole?"

"Yes. This is *Hollywood Tonight*. We were wondering if you had any response to Peter Bianchi's tweeting . . ."

"I don't do Twitter." I hung up.

# CHAPTER EIGHT

was in the kitchen pouring another glass of wine when Deputy Sheriff Ford finally called. I told him what had happened, sounding as discombobulated as the guy with the gun. There was a long pause when I finished.

"Are you there?" I asked.

"You should've called 911 when you had the chance. We might have gotten the guy who was threatening you. Did you get his name?"

"No."

"Make of car? License plate number?"

"No and no."

"Age?"

"Early thirties."

"Appearance?"

"He was the same man who pulled the dead woman's caftan down at the scene of the accident."

There was another long pause. "Can you tell me anything else about him?"

"He wasn't very tall. Maybe five-five. Brown hair carefully combed, leather jacket. Cupid lips."

"Hold on, I'm going to send a patrol car to your area and see if we can still locate him." His voice was replaced by the Beatles singing "The Long and Winding Road." Only in Malibu.

Mindlessly humming along, I stared at my reflection in the window over the kitchen sink. My hair looked as if I'd been racking my hands through it. Had I? My eyes and lips were drawn down. I smiled my professional smile at myself. It made me look worse.

The sheriff's voice replaced the Beatles. "They're on their way. He's probably long gone by now but better safe than sorry."

"He called her Elizabeth," I said. "And he told me they are giving her pills. Who are 'they'?" I asked.

I could hear him breathing. Finally he spoke. "She's been identi- fied as Elizabeth Rodgers. She ran away from a drug rehab center. I'm telling you this because the media has the same information now. Since you're not family I can't say anything else."

"What rehab center?"

He let out a sigh. "StarView."

"He said I could be in danger."

"There is no reason you should be in danger except from him. I'll keep the patrol car in your area for tonight. By the way, how did you do at your reading?"

"What? Oh, I don't know yet."

"I always like to know what my stars are doing in Malibu."

*His stars?* "Sheriff, could we concentrate here?" I heard a sharp intake of his breath. "Why did this man search me out about

Elizabeth Rodgers? And why does he think I have her scorpion? What's going on here?"

"If we find him we'll have that answer, won't we?"

"If?"

"Ms. Poole, we'll keep a look out for him. But you should have called 911 right away. Don't worry and good luck on getting that part." He hung up.

Condescending bastard.

I stared at my reflection again. I might've lost my looks for the moment, but I hadn't lost my brains. None of this felt right. Growing up in Los Angeles, I had seen my share of traffic accidents. People driving too fast, not being able to make the curves on Sunset Boulevard, cutting in and out, crashing into each other. I've gotten calls from lawyers because I was a witness, but never once has somebody come after me with a gun.

I picked up the phone and called Ryan.

"I know her name," I said, when he finally answered.

"Whose?"

"The woman who was haunting you. The dead woman's."

"What is it?" He sounded like he'd been asleep or writing.

"Elizabeth Rodgers. She ran away from a rehab center called StarView not far from us."

"Elizabeth Rodgers."

"Who's Elizabeth?" I heard a female voice ask.

"Christ, are you talking to me while you have someone in bed with you?"

"Can we talk about this tomorrow?"

Irrational anger consumed me. "Do you know what I've just been through while you're screwing some lint head?"

"She not a lint head. She's a yoga teacher," he said in a whisper.

"I was held at gunpoint by the guy that was at the accident who told me some incoherent story. I've been scared out of my wits, and I find out her name so *you* can stop being traumatized . . ."

"You were having a conversation with a guy . . . ?"

"We were not having a conversation. He had a gun. And where were you when I almost got killed?"

"You should've called me. I would have come down."

"You were having sex."

"I was having it now, not then."

"Then you shouldn't have answered the phone."

"I think you and I should go to counseling."

My doorbell rang and I gripped the edge of the sink. "There's someone at the door."

"This isn't the movies, Diana, don't answer it."

"It might be the police. I called the sheriff." I crept toward the foyer.

"Tanya doesn't think you should answer it either."

"*Tanya?*"

There were two hard firm knocks. I froze. Then I forced myself to peer into the peephole. A man stood back from the door wearing a pale blue shirt and darker blue Bermuda shorts. His knees were as white as baseballs. He held a FedEx package in his hand.

I let out my breath. "It's Roy." I disconnected and opened the door.

"Looks like a pair of shoes." Roy liked to guess what was in the boxes he delivered.

I took the package. "Right again. Thanks, Roy."

As he started to leave, he pointed at my brick path. "You dropped something."

I looked down to where he was gesturing. The gun the man had laid on the ground glinted in the light from the porch.

"It's not going to do you much good out here. A lot of my clients have security guards. But they're the big stars, who can afford to have others protect them." Bending down, he picked up the pistol. He waited for me to take it from him.

# CHAPTER NINE

What kind of gunman leaves without his gun? Obviously not a very good one. After bolting the front door, I went into my bedroom and placed the weapon on my bedside table. It looked new. And as he had told me, the safety catch was on. I went back to the kitchen and grabbed another bottle of red, a glass, and returned to the bedroom.

In my bathroom, I washed my face, and slathered on my expensive anti-aging creams. Grabbing my laptop, I got into bed, drank wine, and Googled rehab centers in Malibu. (The irony was not lost on me.) A map came up. Red dots, each representing a rehab center, lined the coast and spread up into the hills of Malibu. There were so many red dots that it looked like a bloodbath. I had read in the local newspapers about the concern about the growing number of clinics taking over our neighborhoods, but I hadn't paid that much attention. God, people couldn't get sober without an ocean view?

Pouring myself another glass, I located StarView on Windswept Road. I had never driven up the road but I knew it well. It had a signal and a crosswalk. Ryan and I used it when we walked across PCH to Kiki's, our local bar. Then I Googled Elizabeth Rodgers. There were many women with that name. And a lot of pictures. But none of them fit her age or description.

I closed the laptop, tossed it to the empty side of the bed, and leaned back into my pillows, sloshing down more vino. Elizabeth Rogers had been living close by in StarView, I thought. And she had a scorpion. Christ. Reaching for the bottle, I stared right into the barrel of the gun on the nightstand. Hell. I could see the headlines: AGING ACTRESS SPURNED BY YOUNG LOVER SHOOTS SELF.

In one of my more rational moves, I checked to see if the gun really was empty. It was. That meant the man didn't mean to harm me. He was just trying to keep me cornered long enough to tell me his rambling story. I downed another glass and decided to phone Deputy Sheriff Ford to tell him I had the guy's weapon. Then I remembered the man's shaking hands and wide eyes. He had been more scared than I was. Also I didn't want to talk to Ford buzzed on wine. Instead, I opened the drawer and placed the weapon inside, wishing I could put the accident and its aftereffects out of my mind as easily.

I took a sleeping pill, turned on the TV, and watched James Gandolfini act his weak heart out in a *Sopranos* rerun.

The next morning, I got out of bed and put on sweat pants and a T-shirt. Pouring some coffee, I walked out onto my deck. The fog was salty and humid. I watched as a man threw a stick the size of small log out into the ocean for his Lab to retrieve. Two middle-aged women walked and talked. Mostly talked. A lone man with a large cigar paced, yelling into his cell phone. He was a high-powered agent who, when younger and without power, had gone to bed with my mother trying to get her for a client. It didn't work.

Below me a woman, in black tights and a skimpy black top, stood on a lavender-colored mat doing the Tree Pose. Her back was to me. But I assumed by her tight ass, small waist, perky ponytail, and the fact she was doing yoga, she must be Tanya. She balanced perfectly on one leg. The other was raised up, knee extending to the side, foot resting high on her inner thigh. Her hands were held over her head. I don't trust people who do yoga in public. It's an exhibition, not meditation.

Ryan padded down his stairs, his matching lavender-colored mat rolled up under his arm, wearing sweats. As he flipped his mat down on the sand next to Tanya, he looked up and saw me.

"Diana, are you all right?"

"Yes."

"I'm sorry about last night."

"Awkward moment, that's all."

"Do you want to talk?" he asked.

"No. Well, there is one thing. The man who held the gun on me said that Elizabeth Rodgers had a scorpion."

"A what?" He squinted up at me.

"He was unclear. In fact he wasn't making sense."

"Do you want to do yoga with us? It'll center you." Tanya said, turning toward me. Beautiful dark eyes slanted toward her shiny black hairline, teeth shined whiter against her latte-colored skin. Tanya looked like she belonged in Bali but sounded like she lived in Marina del Rey in a singles condo with a tiny balcony and a hibachi pot.

"No, thanks." Cupping my coffee mug between my hands, I leaned my arms on the railing. "When did you two meet?"

"Yesterday," she said.

"When I left your house. She was practicing yoga out here." He gestured at the wide expanse of sand. "I was in such a state. And she calmed me down immediately. We spent the whole day and night together."

"Serendipity," she said.

Such a big word, I thought. "I hope my call didn't bring it all back to you, Ryan."

He gave me a quick look to make sure I wasn't being sarcastic. "I thought it would. But Tanya helped me. I didn't dream of her, Diana."

"Tanya?"

"No, the dead woman."

"Elizabeth Rogers. She has a name, now."

"Names are not important. It's the emotion that's important." Tanya looked up at me.

I wanted to puke. "Well, a name can come in handy when you're trying to identify a dead person."

Ignoring me, she turned to Ryan. "Lie down." She pointed to his mat.

Like a good dog Ryan lay on his back as if he were waiting to get his belly scratched.

"Now extend your right leg into the air, sweetie."

Obeying, he groaned. Christ, he still had his Uggs on. His face turned bright red. I felt a pang of separation. In one day Ryan had found a shiny new bauble to keep the twilight of his career away, to keep Elizabeth Rodgers away. Now I was left with her.

# CHAPTER TEN

My cell rang. I hurried back into the house and grabbed it off the coffee table. It was my agent. My heart skipped a beat with hope. He machine-gunned his words into my ear. *Ratta-tat-tat* . . . didn't get the part . . . *ratta-tat-tat* . . . there will be others . . . *ratta-tat-tat* . . . He hung up.

I slumped on the sofa and let out a bitter sigh. Gabrielle Hays, my blond nemesis, got the role. There's an old, old joke about Hollywood. It goes like this: A circus is having a parade down Main Street. A man walks behind the elephants sweeping up their shit. When someone asks him, "Why don't you get a better job?" the man says, surprised, "What, and get out of show biz?"

Well, I couldn't sit here all day. I did have a life to get on with. Depression one sticky step at a time crawled into me, darkening my world. Enough. I'm a pro. I've lost parts before. And I've gotten parts before. I shoved off the sofa and stood for a moment unsure what to do. It was still morning. The day loomed in front of me. And for the first time I questioned whether acting was what I wanted to do with the rest of my life. Stop it. Diana. Do something. I decided to get the *Los Angeles Times*. Yes, I still read ink. Feeling full of fake purpose, I went into the foyer, checked the peephole, and opened the door.

My jaw tightened. A bouquet of flowers, like the one Bianchi had left for me the day of the accident, had been placed on top of the paper. I grabbed it and took the card out from between the petals. It read: *Diana, I'm here for you.*

A perfect storm hit me. The loss of a starring role and an ex-lover who couldn't let go.

Holding the flowers like a club, I ran down my pathway. Anger, rage gave me true purpose.

Peter Bianchi was waiting for me in his black Porsche on the other side of PCH. Cars roared past me. "Stop this, you son of a bitch," I yelled over them, stabbing the air with the bouquet like a maniacal bridesmaid.

There was a break in traffic. I ran. On the embankment, I leaned into his passenger-side window. My heart pounded. Words shot out of me. "Sick bastard. Restraining order. Pervert. What are you doing? Twitterfuck." Running out of air and invective, I stuttered to a stop.

Peter turned his dark romantic face to mine. Black eyes. Full lips. "I'm just sitting in my car on a public highway taking in the glories of Malibu. You know what I discovered? If you look long enough it isn't that attractive. It's like looking at a woman and really seeing her. Without movie stars Malibu is just another funky beach town. Without all the makeup you're just another aging bitch."

Before I could shove the bouquet in his face, he threw his car in gear and sped off leaving me in his dust. Literally.

A death grip on Bianchi's flowers, I let out a deep primordial moan. Cars raced by me spewing bits of gravel and exhaust. Then I saw the debris a few feet from where I stood. I moved closer. Thick pieces of headlights glinted dully among red plastic shards of brake lights and chunks of fenders. Fragments from the accident swept to the side of the road. No spontaneous memorial had been set up for Elizabeth Rogers, no flowers shriveling in the sun, no cute little teddy bears, or votive candles, flames long blown out. Just rubble.

Deciding she needed flowers, I knelt down and placed them on top of the remains of the wreckage. As I started to get to my feet, I noticed something shine with more clarity and determination than the other pieces of scrap. My fingers wedged the object free. It was small and it glittered with a cold relentlessness as only diamonds can.

Standing up, I stared at the scorpion-shaped, diamond-encrusted object. I closed my fingers around its hard stones and sharp edges, feeling its familiar shape in my hand.

# CHAPTER ELEVEN

t's my birth sign, darling," Mother had told me. "A fan gave it to me."

Mother was living alone in the Bel Air Hotel, drinking heavily. I had made one of my infrequent visits to check on her.

"It looks very expensive." I felt the weight of the scorpion bracelet in my palm as I placed it back on her nightstand.

"I think men who give women expensive things are trying to control them." She and the scorpion charm eyed each other. She wore black-framed glasses.

"Does this fan visit you?"

"He wants to take me away from my coffin." She flipped her hand at the beautiful bedroom suite she was spending all her money on.

I stood at the end of her bed. She nestled against a pile of white pillows. Thick blond hair pulled back. Shot glass of bourbon on the nightstand along with the half-empty bottle. My arms were crossed against my chest, angry with her for taking to her bed, for giving up, for living the rest of her life in such a useless way. My mother was many things, but not useless, and I'd never known her to give up.

"Why don't you let him? Why don't you just get out of bed and get on with your life?"

"Age, Diana, it's the great equalizer."

"You know that's bull. Are you going to pawn it?"

"Your mean my lovely gift? I'd have to get out of bed to do that. Unless you'd like to do it for me?"

"No."

Mother didn't own many possessions. She'd sold most of her luxe gifts. "They weigh you down with responsibility and regret," she had explained once. "Hard cash is freedom." Not a sentimental woman.

"I'm going to be on location for the next month, so I'll be out of town," I told her.

"Where? Paris, I hope."

"South Carolina."

"Oh God, not one of these hot Southern movies where you have to tramp through the swamps and talk through your nose."

"You could still be working."

"I've given up, Diana. You're free."

"What does that mean?"

"It means . . . it means I love you." Her frank blue eyes met mine.

I froze. It was not a term I often heard. When I did she made it sound magnanimous. But in the hotel room that day her words stripped us both bare. An aging mother. An aging daughter. One ready to give up the battle. The other not.

Love.

I left, swallowing back my regret. Her angry abandoned child couldn't say the word. It was the last time I saw her.

Of course at the time I didn't know she had slept with my husband. Slept. What a benign euphemism. They didn't sleep. They fucked.

The scorpion shimmered in the sun. It looked as if it was trying to crawl from my hand. Before it could escape, I tucked the bracelet into the zip-pocket of my sweats.

How did Elizabeth Rodgers have this in her possession? I gazed across PCH to my house. She could see me as well as I could see her. Did she know I was Nora Poole's daughter? If so, how did she get the scorpion from my mother? And why did the guy with the gun want it back? Christ, I had never asked my mother the fan's name.

I stared down at the bouquet and the broken pieces of cars. A chill came over me. I remembered Elizabeth Rodgers standing here, turning her head, and watching the Range Rover or SUV pull up onto the embankment. Then she looked back at me and walked into the traffic. What made her to do that? Fear. Fear of who was in the car.

I could go home and get on with my life, my career, sit on the balcony and breathe in the ocean air. Forget about Elizabeth Rodgers. Forget about the diamond-encrusted scorpion in my pocket. I could sell it if I needed money. But I didn't do any of that.

# CHAPTER TWELVE

I turned on my heel and walked down the embankment to the signal. I had no intention of crossing PCH and heading back up to my house. I strode up the newly paved Windswept Road to StarView.

The lots nearest the highway were vacant and overgrown with foxtails swaying in the thinning fog. A child's memory. Running on thin legs, foxtails piercing my white uniform knee socks. The fresh experience of my young breasts rising and falling under my blouse as I hurried toward a boy who was waiting, hands ready. Or was I running toward a place called Yugoslavia where my mother was making a movie? And I was left behind. Again.

At a steep incline I slowed my pace. I was out of shape. Well-kept family homes appeared. I didn't see any children playing in the street. The houses looked shuttered. It felt like a set on a studio's back lot. All façade.

I came to a cul-de-sac. Enormous iron gates stood open to a cobblestone driveway that wound up to a sprawling Cape Cod–style home sitting high on a hill half hidden behind a thick, trimmed green hedge. Above the hedge I could see stark white balconies, green painted shutters, and a green tin roof.

"I've always wondered about something," a female voice said.

Startled, I whipped around and looked into the face of a woman who was in her late thirties and not too happy about it. She held a water bottle in her hand.

"Do you gossip about me the way I gossip about you?" she asked.

"Sorry?" Her skin was lined with anger and her eyes looked like she hadn't slept much. Was she a patient here? "Do we know each other?"

"You don't know me but I know you. I read about you and see you in the movies and on TV." She studied me for a long moment, then said, "I know Peter Bianchi broke up with you. What did you expect? You're too old for him. And why should I have to care about that?" Her voice rose with indignation. "Tell me!" She poked the water bottle at me.

"You don't." Christ, I felt like I had wandered into a Pinter play where only the unspoken subtext had meaning and the director hadn't told me what it was. I grabbed for some kind of reality. "I broke up with Peter."

"Do you care if I broke up with my husband?"

"I don't know your. . . ."

"Exactly. I don't know you either!" She dragged her hand through her hair, the color of *au jus*. "That's not the point. The point is you celebrities can just invade our lives and I'm sick of it. My husband wanted to sell the house to StarView but I wouldn't let him. They offered a lot of money but I stood my ground, saying this is our home. A home!" Spilling water, she jabbed the bottle at me again. I took a step back. "Do you know the meaning of that word *home*?"

"Not really," I said honestly. "And stop poking me with that bottle."

"We worked hard for ours." Tears shined in her eyes. "I'm not going to let them come into my neighborhood and take over with out-of-control celebrities and CEOs arriving in the dark in their limos so they can get sober and turn our neighborhood into an extension of this big spa for the wealthy and the famous. Don't you people care about anybody else except yourselves?"

I edged around the one-woman Greek chorus and started toward the gates.

"They don't take walk-ins." She wiped the back of her hand across her eyes.

"You wanna get clean you have to pay first, sneak in in the dead of night like the others so the paparazzi can't video you. Do you wanna see what your kind has caused? Look around. There's no families living in these homes any more. Just me. I want you to think about what you and your addictions have done to my neighborhood, to my peace of mind, to my life. And if you really want to get clean, go to AA like the real people." She turned to leave.

"Wait, do you know Elizabeth Rodgers?"

"No." She looked back at me.

"You must've of heard of her. She ran away from here three nights ago and got run over on PCH."

Her expression held firm, but something in her eyes, a flicker, of being thrown off her game like an actor on a roll who realized the other actor has forgotten his lines.

"No, I don't." She marched away into her nice lonely house.

Without her yammering, it was eerily quiet except for the distant sound of traffic on PCH and seagulls cawing, scavenging for garbage. The sun had broken through the fog and bleached the moody blue from the ocean, turning it a silvery white. I peered back at the

Cape Cod house. A woman appeared on the balcony in a spa robe. The wind ruffled her henna-red hair as she put a trembling hand to her lips and sucked on a cigarette. After a few long draws she flicked the still-lit cigarette into the garden below and went back into her room.

And then I noticed the security cameras, one on each side of the iron gates. I began to walk up the cobblestone driveway.

# CHAPTER THIRTEEN

I stood at the top of the StarView drive taking in a panoramic view of the jutting, curving coast. An infinity swimming pool looked as if it were going to slip off the property and pour downhill into the distant ocean. Bent toward each other in intense conversation, two men sat on the edges of their lounges. One was young and clad in jeans and a T-shirt. The other was much older with a shock of unruly gray hair, wearing a heavy tweed jacket, which looked about as out of place as if he were clad in a suit of armor. Near the pool was a pristine tennis court with a covered spectator area splashed with red bougainvillea. Beside it was a path through a swath of lawn leading up into the mountains. A small wooden sign declared: WALKING TRAIL.

I felt as if I had stumbled into a very elite resort. Toward the back of the large white Cap Cod house was a parking area with three black Range Rovers. The same make I had seen at the accident. I peered up at an oak tree. A camera, perched like a crow on a limb, peered back down at me. The resort effect vanished.

A golf cart shot around the corner of the house through the parking area and came to a halt in front of me. A young man in a loose white linen shirt and jeans swung out of it. "May I help you?" A bright smile flashed at me. A string of wooden beads with a feather hung around his neck.

"I'm Diana Poole, and I'd like to speak to somebody in charge."

"I'm sorry, but you have to make an appointment. If you're in distress we have a number you can call." He reached into his pocket and came out with a card. I didn't take it.

"I'd like to speak to someone about Elizabeth Rodgers."

By the pool, the man in the tweed jacket had stood up and was watching us.

"Are you family?" the young man asked.

"Elizabeth Rodgers died in front of my house."

"I can't make an exception. Please, get in the cart and I'll drive you back down."

"No."

"Don't force me to call security."

"I thought you were."

"Only the first tier." He flushed.

"How many tiers are there?"

"Three."

"Hot oil? Dogs?"

"You don't want to test our security," he warned.

"If you don't want intruders, why is the gate open?"

"Because our clients aren't prisoners. They're here because they want to be."

The gray-haired man was now walking toward us. We both turned as he approached.

"What's the problem, Eddie?" He raised his dark bushy brows waiting for an explanation. A hawk nose jutted from his cragged face.

"She says she's Diana Poole and wants to . . ."

"I *am* Diana Poole. Elizabeth Rodgers was run over in front of my house. I'd like to talk to someone about it."

He turned to Eddie. "Go up to Decker's office and tell him Diana Poole is waiting to see him." His voice was deep and resonant like a Shakespearean actor. Gray-blue eyes radiated a nonthreatening strength.

"He's with someone."

"Whisper the message in his ear or hand him a note. Be creative."

"But the rules say . . ." Eddie stammered.

He clasped the young man on his shoulder. Man to boy. "This woman is a famous member of the Malibu community. She witnessed a horrific accident. The public relations people will thank you for breaking the rules."

"Yes, sir." Eddie hurried up a flagstone path to a wide porch and disappeared into the house.

The man turned his avuncular eyes on me. "We're a little like the addicts we treat. We don't handle the unexpected well. Marc Decker is the head of StarView. You can't get more in charge than that." He thought a moment. The smile disappeared. "Seeing her death must've been a shattering experience."

"The aftereffects have been pretty shattering too."

"You're having trouble coping? If so, coming here might help."

"That's not what meant. I'm not looking for closure."

"Did I say anything about closure?" Humor glinted in his eyes. "I was thinking more along the lines of perspective."

"Let me guess, you're a therapist."

"Wrong."

"Really?" I was warming to him.

"Psychiatrist. Not the same at all. Many years of medical training and analysis, though I think in this wired age my field is considered anachronistic." He held out his hand. I took it. It was large and warm. "Dr. Sam Walford. Careful when Marc Decker shakes hands with you. He wears a big college ring on his finger. Very proud of it. It can dig into your skin. I'm with a client right now. If I have time, I'll try to join you and Marc, if you don't mind."

"I don't mind."

"You can wait on the porch for Eddie." He strode back to the young man by the pool.

I watched Dr. Walford put a comforting arm around his patient. It took me a moment to realize the young man was sobbing. Feeling as if I was intruding, I turned away, walked up the flagstone path to the porch, and felt its comforting shade.

The French doors opened, and Leo Heath strode out. He stopped dead when he saw me.

And all the air was sucked out of Malibu. Or maybe just out of me.

Straightening his six-foot frame, he jammed his hands into the pockets of his jeans. Under his black tailored jacket he wore a crisp white shirt open at the neck.

He wasn't heavily muscled but he had a matter-of-fact self-possession that implied don't-mess-with-me. Chestnut brown hair, grayer at the temples than I remembered, swept back from his lean, carved face. His crooked nose still looked as if it had taken a few punches. Sunglasses covered what I knew were dark, somber eyes.

I had imagined running into Heath many times. But I was always wearing my sexiest clothes and my highest heels. So of course when it actually happened, I was in sweats, no makeup, and hair uncombed. But I was an actress. I may be in complete disarray, and my heart thudding like a schoolgirl's, but I could take on the demeanor of a woman dripping in Prada and wearing her new Louboutins. I straightened up to all my five-foot-seven inches, put my hand on my hip, tossed my determinedly blond hair, and tilted my chin up to him.

"Hello, Heath." My voice was steady.

"Diana. It's been a long time."

"Are you doing the security for StarView?"

"No."

"So why are you here?"

His serious lips slipped into a crooked smile. "How did we bypass the 'how-are-you's' and the 'what-have-you-been-up-to's'?"

I let out my breath. "How are you?"

"Fine." He hadn't taken off his sunglasses, hadn't looked me in the eyes. Irritating.

"What have you been up to?"

"Same old. Covering security. Working for my clients. In fact, that's why I'm here."

"Let me guess. Your client is some multimillionaire movie star who got sober and discovered he was still an asshole and wants to sue them now."

He took his right hand out of his pocket and rubbed the bump on the ridge of his nose. "I see your view of me hasn't changed."

"My view of your clients hasn't changed."

"Still as righteous as ever, even with a little dirt on you."

I glanced down at my sweat pants. Christ, my knees were filthy from kneeling on the side of the highway.

Eddie burst out onto the porch. "Sorry for all the confusion. Mr. Decker will meet with you now."

"Well, I'll be going. See you around, Diana."

Heath loped down the porch steps and then ambled down the driveway. Watching, I wondered why he hadn't asked me what I was doing at StarView.

"We have to be careful," Eddie was yakking behind me. "Fans, paparazzi, even friends like to sneak in and see our clients. Sometimes they bring them . . . things. You know."

"How many patients do you have?" I asked, letting out my breath as Heath disappeared from sight.

"Never more than ten. And we don't call them patients."

I turned and looked into Eddie's eyes. Pool boy eyes. Faded blue. Too much sun. "What do you call them?"

"Clients."

"Why?"

"I don't know. Maybe because everybody's so important."

"Was Elizabeth Rodgers important?"

His face went blank. "This way."

I followed him into what could only be called the great room. Running the length of the entire house, it had floor-to-ceiling windows. All the light of Malibu poured in through them. Giant stone fireplaces covered the walls at each end of the room. The wood floors were polished dark with expensive rugs scattered everywhere. Leather sofas and chairs, a cool forest-green color, were grouped for conversation.

A man about my age, looking as if he owned the place, sprawled on one of the sofas reading *You'll Never Eat Lunch in This Town Again*. I knew him. We had a brief affair at the beginning of our careers. That was after my mother had an affair with him. Now he was an executive producer at Sony Pictures who never hired me. He peered over the rim of his book with deadened eyes. A flick of his eyebrow conveyed acknowledgment, I think, then he went back to his book.

A girl in her twenties stood at a round table cutting the stems off flowers with blunted scissors. An older woman in a linen shirt and trousers helped her place the flowers in a vase. She also wore a beaded necklace with a feather.

"Very good," she said to the young woman. "See? It doesn't hurt the flowers."

Through an arch was a dining room. A young man in a white *dishdasha* shirt fondled worry beads with long delicate fingers as he whispered to another man. The conversation looked more conspiratorial than cathartic.

The girl with flowers gasped loudly, sending a shudder through the quiet, perfect room.

Disgusted, the executive producer tossed his book on a coffee table, swung his legs off the sofa. "I have one fucking hour to myself, and I have to put up with this." He stomped out of the room, slamming the door. Once an executive producer, always an executive producer.

The girl stared at me with wide, haunted eyes, one hand pressed on her right breast as if it hurt her. I looked down at the table and saw a milky white substance ooze from the stem she had just cut.

"That's natural for these kinds of flowers to do that," her attendant cooed.

The girl's face distorted with grief. The substance looked like mother's milk, I thought. She's lost a baby. Make the connection, you idiot, I wanted to yell at the attendant. But Eddie had a firm hand on my elbow and was propelling me up a sweep of stairs. I told myself to quit projecting. Mother. Loss. Loss. Mother. It had to be the damn scorpion in my pocket.

# CHAPTER FOURTEEN

At the top of the landing, Eddie knocked on a door.

A voice commanded, "Come."

Eddie opened the door. I went in, and he left, closing it softly behind me.

A man, in his mid fifties, dressed in an expensive tailored dark gray suit, stood up from behind his desk. He was tall, elegant, and wore a teal blue tie that matched his teal blue eyes. He moved gracefully to me. He was the kind of man who made a woman feel underdressed instead of undressed.

"Diana Poole? Marc Decker." He offered his hand. I took it. Dr. Sam Walford's warning came back to me as the man's heavy gold ring with a ruby stone dug into my fingers. I tried not to grimace as he added more pressure. This wasn't a handshake, it was a sadistic exercise in power.

"Nice ring," I said. "High school?"

He dropped my hand. "Oxford," he said coldly. Then he threw his head back and laughed. "I must apologize. Sam Walford keeps telling me to get rid of it. He says it represents a need to be a part of an elite group. But then I tell him I am."

I wanted information so I tried to be nicer. "Were you a Rhodes scholar?"

"I was." He seemed impressed I knew such things. "Please, sit down."

He gestured to a chair in front of his desk, a large slab of brown, black, and gray marble balanced on brass legs. He rested his hip on the edge of it, looking down his patrician nose at me.

"It's a pleasure to meet you," he continued. "I've seen quite a few of your movies, and your mother's too. In fact, when I was a young man I thought your mother was the most beautiful woman I'd ever seen."

"You met her?"

"Only on screen."

"You were a fan."

"I suppose you could say that."

I smiled. "You must deal with a lot of famous people."

"Yes, I do." He paused glancing at his watch. "You were lucky to catch me in. I was leaving to fly up to Mendocino. We're opening a new clinic in the Sonoma wine country."

"What do the vineyards think of that?" I smiled.

"I never thought to ask them." Decker blinked at me. He had no sense of humor. I don't like humorless men. "What can I do for you, Ms. Poole?"

"I witnessed Elizabeth Rodgers's death."

"I'm so sorry. We're all shaken by that event."

Tired of looking up at him, I stood and walked to a window and peered out. Any good actor learns when to pause in a scene and when not to. I paused, watching two women and a man doing yoga. Then I turned away from the window and met his waiting eyes.

"The night after the accident a man who knew Elizabeth Rodgers held me at gunpoint," I told him.

He showed no reaction. Maybe I didn't pause long enough.

"The man has dark hair. Cupid lips. He's not very tall. Small hands."

Expressionless, he stared at me.

"He thought I had something. A scorpion bracelet. He told me Elizabeth Rodgers had wanted me to see it. Or some woman. He was vague. I didn't know what he was talking about. Eventually I got into my house and called Deputy Sheriff Ford."

"And what do you want from me, Ms. Poole?"

"He also told me that you were overmedicating Elizabeth Rodgers. So I thought he might work for you. Her attendant, maybe. I would like to talk to him."

"We do have an attendant who answers to that description, but he would never hold a gun on anybody."

"May I have his name?"

"I can't do that. We are bound by privacy agreements that protect our clientele. And our counselors and attendants also sign agreements that prevent them from talking about StarView." Decker stood and adjusted his jacket. "And we use medication to help some of our clients transfer from addiction to sobriety, but it's very controlled and not an unusual practice. I'm sorry I can't help you. But as I said, I have plane to catch."

I unzipped my pocket and took out the bracelet. The diamond-encrusted scorpion swayed from its chain as I set it on his desk. Brows knitted, Decker peered at it as if he wished he had a can of Raid, then looked at me, waiting for an explanation.

"I found this in the debris from the accident."

"And?"

"And I think Elizabeth Rodgers had this in her hand when she was waving at me. I think she wanted me to see it or maybe give it to me. I also believe that this bracelet was what your attendant wanted."

There was a knock on the door and it opened. Dr. Sam Walford stuck his head in. "Mind if I join you?" He walked in, not waiting for an answer.

Decker's shoulders tensed, then relaxed. He shoved his hands into his pants pockets and walked toward the window, turned, and walked back. He looked as if he was modeling his suit. Walford stared at the glittering object on the desk as if he had been struck by something.

"Amazing how there can be beauty in such garishness." He blinked, looking up at Decker and me. "What is it? A scarab?"

"A scorpion," I said. "I don't think a scarab has much of a tail. I thought a man of your intelligence might know the difference."

"Where creepy crawlies are concerned my mind is reduced to a five-year-old's."

I smiled. "It belonged to my mother. It was her birth sign. A fan gave it to her."

"Your mother?" Walford's bushy eyebrows arched. For a moment he looked lost.

"Nora Poole," Decker snapped. "I thought you said it belonged to Elizabeth Rodgers."

"No. I said she had it when she died. How she got it from my mother, I don't know. I found it on the side of the highway near the accident."

"I was told many cars were involved in the mishap," Decker said. "It might have come from any one of them."

"The odds of that would be even more astounding." Walford handed the bracelet back to me.

"That's another thing that bothers me," I said. "I don't think it was an accident."

"But you said you witnessed it," Walford said.

Decker's face tensed. "What else could it have been?"

"I mean it was. But one of your Range Rovers pulled off the highway. The passenger door opened. That's when Elizabeth Rodgers walked right into the traffic."

"Are you saying she would rather have died than be brought back to StarView? That's going too far, Ms. Poole. Her attendant was only trying to help her. And I can assure you they liked each other and got along well."

"He cared for Elizabeth a great deal." Walford was the only person to use her first name. He made her sound as if she had a life.

"Maybe she was afraid of the person driving the car," I said.

Questioning, Walford turned to Decker.

Decker smoothed his tie. "There was nobody else in the Rover, Ms. Poole. I've checked with all my employees. I hope you take what I'm about to say as an attempt to help you. You've had two traumatic experiences this week. You're a sensitive actress. Seeing a woman run over and killed must have disturbed you deeply. And being rejected by that younger actor—*Peter Bianchi*—could easily have been as hard on you."

"Peter Bianchi? I thought you might want to help."

"I'm only saying that these two events could lead you to search for answers or conclusions that just don't exist." He looked me up and down, taking in my dusty appearance. "Even act in odd ways. And I can assure you there is nobody at StarView who wanted to harm Elizabeth Rodgers."

"Marc," Walford cut in. "Why don't you leave the psychiatric observations to me? Weren't you going to fly up to Mendocino? I'll walk Ms. Poole down. Try to get some sleep on the plane."

Decker frowned. Then he rubbed a hand over his face. The ruby stone in his ring flickered darkly. "I guess I've been more affected by her death than I realized." An old battle or emotion, nothing to do with the moment, hung in the air between the two men.

Feeling the sharp edges of the scorpion, I let the bracelet slip from my hand back into my pocket.

# CHAPTER FIFTEEN

D r. Walford walked me down the stairs to the great room. The young woman I saw earlier cutting flowers was now leaning on the table sobbing. Eddie and the girl's attendant were on their knees picking up pieces of a broken vase, and flowers.

"Hey, what's going on here?" Walford hurried over to them.

"She's had a hiss tizzy." Fed up, the attendant struggled to her feet.

Ignoring her, Walford turned to the distraught woman. "Now that's a concise diagnosis. Did you have a hiss tizzy?" He grinned and cupped her cheek in his large hand. She sniffled.

Then he ordered Eddie, "Take Ms. Poole out to the porch. I'll drive her down to the gate."

Once outdoors, I took in a deep breath to break up the emotions and tension emanating from the great room and my meeting with Decker.

"They call him the Healer," Eddie said,

"Dr. Walford? Does he like to be called that?"

"He hates it, but it's true. Without him there would be no Star-View. They come worldwide to get his help. But he can't drive the golf cart without putting everyone in danger. So hold on."

I laughed. "Well, at least he's human."

"I think that's his secret."

"Being human?"

"Being like the rest of us. But not. You know?"

"I think so. What about Decker?"

Eddie's eyes became hooded and he clammed up. Was he afraid of Decker? Or something else?

Walford walked out onto the porch, rubbing his hands together. "Ready for a little ride? I'll take your cart, Eddie."

"Yes, sir. Do you remember where the brake is?"

"Are you trying to frighten Ms. Poole?"

"No, sir. Just want to keep you in one piece," he spoke in a proprietary voice.

Winking at me, Walford said, "They worry about me around here. Hop in."

I did. He started the cart, and we shot off down the drive. I gripped the edge of my seat, my head went back, and the wind blew through my hair. The cart bumped and skidded over the cobblestone drive. Grinning like a kid, he took the curves never slowing until we came to a whiplash-stop at the gates.

He turned to me, hair wild, eyes shining. "You have to admit that was fun."

"If you're a twelve-year-old," I said through gritted teeth.

A booming Falstaffian laugh escaped him. It felt forced. Too hardy. "Doesn't hurt to act twelve now and then." He rubbed his hands together and let out a sigh. He looked beyond the iron gates as if he wanted to keep driving forever.

"May I ask you a question?" I pushed hair out of my face. "Is it possible that Elizabeth feared the person driving the Range Rover more than she did dying on Pacific Coast Highway?"

"Decker said her attendant was driving."

"But he got out on the passenger's side. I saw her face. Saw her make the decision. Was she suicidal?"

"Elizabeth was riddled with guilt."

"So are many of us. Is there such a thing as forced suicide?"

"Where did you hear that?"

"In the movies. I played the sister of a woman who was forced to kill herself because she was afraid of the alternative."

"Then you might say every suicide is forced." He studied me, taking in every inch of my face until I felt awkward and glanced away. "Sometimes people are left with very few choices," he added, then his professional demeanor kicked in. "Sorry, I can't tell you more."

"The young patient with the flowers?"

"Yes?"

"Did she lose a baby?"

Surprised, he sat back. "Do you know her?"

"No."

"Yes, she did. She turned to booze and pills to deal with her loss. How did you know?"

"The way she put her hand on her breast when she was cutting the stem, the milky substance."

"You're very empathic."

"Part of being an actress. I'll remember the gesture. Use it in a part maybe."

"Do me a favor and use it in your life." He paused, thinking, then said, "I respect the work we do at StarView. I'm protective of it. I know many Malibu rehab centers have a bad reputation. But here we do help people. Maybe one day that young woman will stay sober and be able to have another baby." He stuck out his hand. "It was a pleasure meeting you, Ms. Poole."

His hand was big and warm on my mine. I got out of the cart. "You never asked about my mother."

He frowned. "I don't understand . . ."

"When most people find out Nora Poole's my mother, they ask about her or tell me how much they loved her."

"I thought you might have put up with enough of that in your life." He grinned, then turned the cart sharply. I leaped out of the way. The cart tilted on two wheels, balanced, and he sped back up the driveway.

I walked down Windswept Road past the empty houses. Soon I was running, and all I could think of was Elizabeth Rodgers, her feet slapping against the pavement, the diamond-encrusted scorpion in her hand, running to her death.

# CHAPTER SIXTEEN

Christ, I left my front door open. I scooped up the *Los Angeles Times* from my doorstep and went into the living room. Ryan was sitting on my sofa sucking on a bottle of beer. His lavender yoga mat was rolled up and rested across his knees. The smell of coffee brewing wafted from the kitchen.

"I have something to tell you." He blinked his golden red eyelashes.

"You made me coffee? Thanks. I have something to show you. And you'll never guess who I ran into." I tossed the paper on the floor then unzipped my pocket and let the bracelet slide off my fingers onto the table.

Ryan leaned forward. The yoga mat slipped from his lap, forgotten. "Nora kept that on her nightstand. She never wore it."

"You recognize it," I said with relief and sat in my new chair. "Do you remember who gave it to her?"

"A fan. She never said his name. But it was a man, by the way she talked."

"Coffee's ready." Leo Heath, sounding like the perfect wife, stood in the kitchen doorway. His jacket was off, my dishtowel tossed over his shoulder. The sleeves of his white shirt were rolled above his wide strong wrists, the Colt dark in his belt holster.

"If I remember, you like your coffee black," he continued as if he always emerged from my kitchen.

"What the hell is going on?" I looked from a nonchalant Heath to a flushed-faced Ryan. Guilt always made him turn red.

"That's what I wanted to tell you." Ryan stood. "Now don't get upset."

"I'm not upset." I tried to control the anger in my voice.

"Remember when I was so traumatized after the accident?" Ryan spoke in a hurried voice. "Well, I called Heath and asked him to look into it for me."

"You hired him?" I lost control. "Why didn't you tell me?"

We were speaking as if Heath wasn't there leaning against the doorjamb, looking sexy as hell. Until I turned on him. "And why didn't you tell me when we bumped into each other at StarView?"

"It's private information. You know that. It's up to Ryan to inform who he wants to."

"And we haven't talked in a year and now you're making me coffee in my own kitchen, in my own house? And I take milk, not black!" I turned back on Ryan. "We'll discuss this outside." I shoved him through the open French doors and slammed them shut behind us.

"I knew you'd act this way," Ryan snapped, the breeze ruffling his red curls. "That's why I didn't tell you."

"Did you set this up to get Heath and me back together?"

"No. It's not about you, Diana. It's about me. I was going crazy. Elizabeth Rodgers was haunting me. I had to get rid of her. So I called Heath and then I met Tanya on the beach all in the same day, and I felt less haunted." He grinned sheepishly. "Then I thought Heath could help you."

"How could he help me?"

"I became less obsessed with Elizabeth Rodgers, and you became more."

"I'm not obsessed with her. Not in the way you think."

"I told him everything you told me. He just wants to interview you and then he'll be on his way."

"To solve the case."

"To find out why that woman walked into traffic. Right in front of us."

"I already know why she did. At least some of it."

"Great, then tell him, and he'll be out of your life."

"I'm not turning this case over to him."

"What case? You're not a private detective. He is."

"He's a Hollywood fixer."

"He has a license. It's what he does. Let him do it."

"He and I worked together to find out who killed that young actress. He wouldn't have solved it without me." Christ, I was sounding righteously indignant. A voice I loathed.

Ryan stared out at the ocean. "I look back on that time when the three of us were together, and I sometimes think that was the best thing that happened to me."

"You ended up in the hospital. You almost died," I reminded him.

"You can pick anything apart." He smiled. "Besides, it's better this way. Tanya says the quicker we let go of Elizabeth, the sooner we can get on with our lives."

I was off again. "That little fuckfest wandering the beach in her Lululemon see-through yoga pants is now your life coach?"

"You above all people should know how hard it is for a beautiful woman to be taken seriously. And I'm fine with what Tanya is." He winked lasciviously.

"You don't even know her."

"That's the point. Why do I have to *know* her?"

Giving up, I leaned against him and watched a seal pop its head up in the distance, all shiny with sun and salty water. Ryan put his arm around me. Now the seal floated on his back, belly basking in the sunshine.

"Okay," I said. "If I'm going to tell Heath what I know, it's going to be on my terms this time. Not his, like last time."

I opened the door for Ryan and we went back in.

Heath was leaning against the fireplace mantel, dishtowel gone, mug in hand. He had put another mug on the side table next to the sofa.

Ryan stood awkwardly between us.

"Do I live or die?" he asked me, head tilted.

"Depends if you can follow a few ground rules." I sat and took a sip of the coffee. Damn, it was good. Ryan planted himself in my new chair. I wondered when it would stop being new.

"Just answer my questions, Diana, and I'll be gone," Heath said.

"No, you won't, because all the answers will keep coming back to my mother, which means to me."

His dark eyes grew alert. "What do you know?"

"Here are the ground rules. First, you can't have other clients who are or were involved with StarView in any way."

"I told you that earlier."

"No, you told me there was no unhappy sober movie star. There could be a producer, a director, a criminal sleazebag."

"Diana . . ." Ryan warned, then grabbed his beer off the coffee table and took a long swallow.

"Ryan, I have to know which side Heath is on this time. I was never sure the last time we worked together."

Heath had that look that said nobody else existed, that he was seeing right through you. It was an expression that usually preceded some form of violence. At one time it had frightened me, but I held my ground now and stared at him.

His too-serious lips slowly opened into a half smile.

"All right," he said. "Ryan is my client. I am not representing anyone else as far as I know that is or has ever been connected with StarView."

"Second rule. We share information equally."

Heath rubbed the bump on the bridge of his nose. "Are you saying you want to work together again?"

"It has nothing to do with 'want.' If you need my information, you have to work with me."

"We haven't talked in almost a year."

"Well then, I guess we'll have to start. I see no reason for us to keep bumping into each other while we're trying to solve the same murder."

His eyebrows shot up. "Murder?"

"Who said anything about murder?" Ryan gaped at me.

"Probably 'forced suicide' is a more accurate description, but it's the same thing in my mind." I focused in on Heath. "Do you agree to both of my conditions?"

Heath's eyes rested on mine. "Yes. Tell me what you know, Diana." He set his coffee on the mantel then took his notepad from his back pocket and flipped it open. Imprinted on the leather cover was the impressive insignia of the U.S. Army. After the World Trade Center and the Pentagon were attacked, Heath had joined and been assigned to the CIU, Criminal Investigative Unit for the army, which served him well now as a Hollywood PI.

I described everything that had happened, from the accident to finding the bracelet and talking with Decker. I left out Peter Bianchi. He listened with a dark intensity, now and then jotting down notes.

When I finished, he studied me for a moment then asked, "Do you want to tell me anything else?"

"No, that's all there is. Now tell us what you know."

"Gerard Quincy is on the run."

"Who's he?" I asked.

"Elizabeth Rodgers's attendant at StarView."

"Did Decker tell you his name?"

"No. I visited the woman who lives next to StarView."

"Angry woman?" I asked, remembering her tirade.

"That's her." He flipped through some note pages. "Her name is Barrie Singer. She and Gerard shared small talk while she was getting her mail or he was taking a walk on his lunch hour."

"I can't believe she can do small talk. Did she know anything about Elizabeth Rodgers?"

"She told me she didn't. StarView frowns on the patients talking to her. But she still has managed to chat with Eddie, one of the security guards."

Heath turned another page. "Gerard Quincy lives in Oxnard. Has a white Ford pickup. I sent one of my agents to check on him. None of his neighbors had seen him since the night of the accident. My guy carefully and unethically entered Quincy's apartment. It looked as if he hadn't slept or eaten there for a while."

"Why is he on the run?" Ryan asked.

Heath closed his notepad. "In my experience, there are only three reasons a person runs. He's afraid for his life. He's guilty of a crime. Or he has a backpack full of what someone else wants. Sometimes it's all three."

Putting his notepad back in his pocket, he moved to the table and picked up the bracelet. "Looks as if the scorpion's on a leash," he said, referring to the gold-link chain. "When is the last time you two saw this?"

"In Nora's bedroom about a month before she died." I looked at Ryan.

"It was always there," he said. "She liked to look at the scorpion. When she died, I assumed it got swept up with the rest of her things. Packed away."

"Did you go through her belongings, Diana?" Heath laid the bracelet down.

"No. They're in Colin's office."

"The scorpion must be worth close to fifty thousand dollars," Heath decided. "But neither of you bothered to find out where it was or who might have taken it after she died?"

Ryan and I glanced at each other like spoiled rich children.

Ryan said, "I have to admit I'd been drinking when taking care of her things."

"It's okay, Ryan," I said, then looked at Heath. "I was on location when Ryan was doing what I should've done. Okay?"

Shrugging, he moved back to the mantel and leaned against it. "You're going to have to find a safe place to put that bracelet. Do you want me to take it?"

"I have a very secure place, and it's not in my house. I'll go through my mother's things tonight." My voice was confident. But the thought of searching the past filled me with dread.

"There has to be a connection between Nora and Elizabeth Rodgers," Ryan said.

Heath looked at him. "Was there a doctor who attended her at the end?"

"Her own doctor. The hotel doctor."

"Can you remember his name?"

Ryan shook his head. "He was Indian."

"I have her death certificate." I hurried into the bedroom. My desk was wedged under the window next to my chintz chair. I pulled out the bottom drawer, searched through it, and found it. There it was. Official. A bureaucratic acknowledgment. Stamped. My mother had died.

Back in the living room, I handed it to Heath. "Dr. Vijay Patel."

"Do you remember anything about him?" he asked Ryan.

"Good guy. Had a drink with me in the bar when they were taking her body away. I broke down. I couldn't . . ."

He dropped his head into his hands. I went to him and put my arm around his shoulders.

Finally he continued, "I went back to the hotel about two weeks after she died. I'm not sure why, just to talk to him. But he'd quit. They wouldn't tell me where he'd gone. He was a good doctor. Your mother trusted him, Diana."

"I'll find him," Heath said, looking at his watch. "I gotta go. Would you mind walking me to the door, Diana?"

Ryan raised his eyebrows at me as I walked with Heath out of the room.

In the foyer, we faced each other in the dim light.

"I thought we were going to share information equally." His dark eyes never left mine.

"We are." I held his gaze.

"Something doesn't ring true in what you've told me."

"Like what?"

"You said you a saw a woman run over on PCH."

"Yes."

"And this morning you grab some flowers you just happened to have lying around and run across the same PCH, with the same heavy traffic, in order to place them where the same woman had once stood."

"You don't think I'm capable of such emotion?"

"I don't think you're capable of that kind of recklessness unless something or someone made you very angry." He shifted his weight. "I've seen you in action. Remember?"

"The point is I found the scorpion bracelet."

"The point is why would you be angry and holding flowers at the same time?"

I thought of the bouquet Peter Bianchi had left on my door-step. I thought of him sitting in his car across PCH watching my house. Watching me. I remembered the rage that had filled me.

"I'll call you if I find something important in my mother's things," I said.

He rolled his shoulders. "Your rules." He opened the door and left. I leaned against it and closed my eyes. Oh, hell.

# CHAPTER SEVENTEEN

The clothes of the dead break your heart.

Late that night I sat on the floor of Colin's office staring at the last of the boxes to be searched. The familiar lifeless air filled the room. On Colin's desk stood his two Oscars, each for Best Screenplay, and my mother's for Best Actress. They made a happy gold-dipped family.

A bottle of Courvoisier sat next to me. I was drunk. It was the only way I could do this.

I peered around at all the boxes I had already sorted through. Their flaps stood upright in brittle surprise that they'd finally been untaped. I'd found nothing. Nothing. Nothing. Nothing.

There were clippings of Mother when she was young and smiling for anything, anyone, working her way up to the top. Then I was there. A little girl, a similar smile, similar blond hair. My head down. Shy. Then the little girl was a lonely teenager. I hadn't gotten control of my hair, but my body bloomed with a growing power. Photos of men appeared in our lives. The men we began to sexually compete for. I wasn't shy anymore. Suddenly I was a woman standing next to an older woman. How many lives had I shed to get to where I am, I wondered. How many had she? I took another swig.

I hated the smell of old newspaper clippings, faded Polaroids, and creased letters. I hated the thought of people smiling in photographs who would in the future, which is now the past, turn around and betray, hurt, and abandon you. I didn't want to see the pictures of friends and relatives who died too young, like my father, or the drooling farts who should have died but have clung on into their old age like misers. I slugged more brandy.

My mother's dresses and suits were neatly folded in the box.

I placed a hand on the pink Chanel suit she hadn't worn for years. Once on a sweater of Colin's I'd found a strand of my hair intertwined with his. I must have rested my head there for comfort, love, sex, or just conversation.

I smelled her suit. Her Givenchy perfume still clung to it. Light and airy. I took another slug of brandy and eyed the clock on Colin's desk. Two in the morning. Fuck. I eyed the bottle. Half empty. Double fuck.

I leaned on the box. I dug deeper through the chic clothes and felt the silky robe at the bottom. I tugged it out. It was stained with food and booze. Smelled of sweat, vomit, illness. Desperation. Is this what the end of life smells like?

I downed another slug. Wondering if I was going to be able to get to my feet, I balled the robe up to stuff it back in with her other clothes. I felt something in the pocket. Slipping my hand into it,

I came out with a crumpled photograph and smoothed it out. Recent. Before she took to her bed. My mother and me. On the beach. Holding hands. I could feel the warmth of her palm cupping mine. I finally found something. A clue. I wanted to say it out loud to someone. Anyone. A clue!

Me in her pocket.

# CHAPTER EIGHTEEN

Only one thing is worse than a major hangover, and that is driving around Beverly Hills looking for a parking place. The next morning, I had one and was doing the other. Behind my sunglasses my eyes were red and raw. My head thumped. The sun bounced off the expensive stores lining Rodeo Drive.

Next to me a kid with a man-bun, or in this case a boy-bun, drove a brand-new Mercedes convertible, his rap music blaring. Affluenza at work. Of course the whole world wanted to hear his playlist. I thought of telling him to turn it down, but I saw a car pull out from a parking place. I gunned mine, cut the kid off, and slipped into the slot. Then I leaned my forehead against the steering wheel and hoped my stomach would settle and the fine sheen of sweat covering my face and hands would slowly evaporate. I never wanted to hear the word Courvoisier again.

When I had finally awakened this morning, I'd called Heath and told him I'd found nothing in my mother's possessions. I left out being drunk, having a crying jag, and the photo that caused it.

Now I dug into my purse, searching for a loose credit card. I touched the scorpion bracelet wrapped safely in cotton, then I found my credit card. I eased gingerly out of my car so I wouldn't rattle my brains. At the parking meter I inserted the card while leaning against it for support. I learned that I had this small piece of Beverly Hills for one whole hour, and the cost was equal to the mortgage on my house.

Across the street was the Bank of Beverly Hills, my destination. Because it was a discreet building, it stood out like an unmanicured thumb among the overly designed shops screaming, "I'm chic!" I took a deep breath and stepped into the crosswalk. Nobody stopped. I edged farther away from the curb. A hot roller slammed on its brakes. The car heaved impatiently. I crept forward as cars swept by me. Triumph! I made it to the other side in one piece, head pounding.

In this town everybody thinks they're more important than every other person. This leads to a narcissistic anarchy. In the chaos of egos, pedestrians are the lowliest form. What do you mean by walking? What kind of image is that? You're embarrassing us.

On the fifth floor of the bank building, I opened the door of Moss & Beckett Fine Art and Jewelry Resold. An armed guard greeted me with a curt smile. The beige carpet had a quiet calmness, like undisturbed sand. A glass showcase ran along one long wall displaying glittering jewels and watches. The walls were covered with paintings from the Impressionists to the contemporary. The jewelry and the artwork once belonged to the famous, the wealthy, the important people. Now they were just people who were in trouble. I was in one of the most exclusive pawnshops in Southern California.

"Diana." Mr. Moss came from around the counter and took my hand. His pale skin looked as if it never felt the California sun. His hair was dyed Elvis-black. He wore a trim dark suit. "So good to see you. Please, this way." He spoke in a hushed voice. Guiding me though a velvet curtain into a corridor, he opened the door of one of the private rooms where price, need, and hopelessness could be talked about securely.

"Please sit down. It's been years since I've seen you. So sorry about your mother."

"Thank you." I sat in front of a gilded desk. A small black velvet pad graced its top.

"Can I get you anything? Coffee? Champagne? Water? We only have still." He sat opposite me.

Shaking my head, I reached into my purse, took out the bracelet, and unwrapped it. The dangling diamond-encrusted scorpion shimmered as I placed it on the pad.

"It belonged to my mother."

Moss adjusted his jeweler's loupe and surveyed every inch of the object. "Quite stunning, but no jeweler's mark." He leaned back in his chair, set the glass on the desk, rubbed his eye.

"How much is it worth?"

"The diamonds are exquisite. But an arthropod isn't the prettiest of creatures. I'd say fifteen to twenty thousand. I'd have to talk to my partner Beckett if you want a direct buyout." He was lowballing me in the most elegant way.

"No, I want to pawn it."

"Five thousand is all I can give you." He held up his hands in a helpless gesture.

"That's fine."

"Done?" He gave a faint chuckle, opened a drawer, and slipped out the contract for me to sign. "Your mother would've gotten another five thousand out of me."

I smiled. "I just want it to be safe. Where will you keep it?"

"Of course you do. It'll be in the bank's vault."

"And I want to make it clear that nobody picks this up but me."

He straightened. "We'd never allow such a thing unless they had your power of attorney. Excuse me, I'll make arrangements for your payment." He moved to the door as if he were afraid to disturb the air. A Mont Blanc pen rested on the contract. I read through it and signed where highlighted.

I had finished when Moss returned.

"It'll be just a few minutes." He settled behind his desk and let out a sigh. "The inscription doesn't relate to your mother. The piece must've been bought from an estate."

"What inscription?" I asked sharply.

"Sorry, I assumed you knew. I mean, because it belonged to Nora."

"I didn't see one. Where is it?"

He turned the shimmering arthropod over. "It's difficult to see." He picked up his loupe and handed it to me. I peered through it.

He pointed with the nib of the Mont Blanc to a curved segment of the tail. "Right there."

"To B. Your B," I read out loud. "I thought it was marring." I handed his glass back to him. "You mean this could have belonged to someone else before it was given to my mother?"

"Yes."

There was a discreet knock on the door.

"Come in, Priscilla," Moss called out.

A woman in dark navy scurried in and placed a gray velvet box in front of me, then hurried out.

Reaching into a desk drawer, Moss pulled out a small gray-colored shopping bag. He put the velvet box into the bag. "Your identification number for this lovely piece is in the box along with your payment." By identification number he meant pawn ticket.

I stood and took the bag. "Thank you."

"And don't worry. It will be safe and secure." He walked me to the door. "Of course they might have had special names for each other."

"Who?"

"Your mother and whoever loved her."

"Loved her?"

Moss was almost dreamy. "The person who gave her this stunning piece of jewelry."

I stumbled out of the bank building. I had never thought of love.

# CHAPTER NINETEEN

W here are you, Heath?" I was on my cell, sitting in my Jag, watching the parking meter tick down to the last few minutes. I wanted my money's worth of Beverly Hills.

"Outside the Holiday Inn off Sunset in Brentwood. Near the freeway."

"Stakeout?"

"Horny wife screwing her hairdresser. This is Rodriquez's case. One of my agents. He's at the dentist with a root canal."

"Will I ruin your cover if I meet you there? I pawned the bracelet at Moss & Becket. I want you to keep the ticket and the money I got for it."

"What cover? The hairdresser and the wife are in a room now. I'm the man in the black Escalade with private detective written all over it. You can't miss me."

I laughed. "See you in a few minutes."

The Holiday Inn was a giant cylinder built high above the 405 freeway. It looked like a silo for storing humans instead of corn.

Heath was parked across the street from the front door of the hotel. I pulled into the parking lot and got out of my car. Carrying the chic gray shopping bag, I walked toward his Escalade. I knew he was observing me behind his sunglasses. At least I wasn't in sweats. I was in my usual jeans and a white silk shirt. The idea of him watching me woke up my dormant sexual needs. Let it go, Diana.

As I reached the passenger door, he leaned over and opened it for me. I climbed in and pulled it shut.

"So are you breaking up a marriage or holding one together?" I greeted.

He rubbed his chin with his hand. "The wife is driving our client nuts. And he's already crazy to begin with."

"Anybody I know?"

"Not unless you go to a lot of lap dancing clubs." He peered over the rim of his sunglasses at me, eyes challenging mine. "In your words, a sleazebag. My client owns a slew of clubs so he can afford to live in Brentwood. Or anywhere else he wants."

Ignoring his challenge, I asked, "Is his wife one of his ex-dancers?"

"She quit when they got married." He gestured toward the hotel. "He thinks she's up there giving lap dances away for free."

"Who's the hairdresser?"

"Roget. Or as our client calls him, Ro . . . get."

"Roget. He gives great highlights. And he's wonderful in bed. So I hear." I batted my lashes and stretched sexily.

"I'll have Rodriquez put that in his report," he said wryly.

"Here." I handed him the shopping bag. "There's five thousand in the velvet jewelry case along with the pawn ticket. You sure it'll be safe with you?"

"I'm sure."

"There's an inscription on the scorpion."

"I didn't see anything."

"You need a jeweler's loupe. It's on the inside curve of the tail."

He took his sunglasses off, tossed them onto the dashboard, and turned in his seat to face me. "What's it say?"

"'To B. Your B.' It could be an estate piece, the initials belonging to the previous owner or owners."

"Does it mean anything to you?"

"No. But Moss of Moss & Becket said that maybe they were short for love names. Who knew he's a romantic."

He frowned. "Meaning, maybe it wasn't a fan but a lover that gave your mother the bracelet?"

"Or maybe my mother didn't return the fan's love."

"But she kept the bracelet, Diana."

"He had to know her birth sign was Scorpio. Then again if it was an estate piece, B and B could be from a long time ago."

"What's wrong?" he asked, studying my face.

"I'm not sure. But I feel as if the inscription has changed something, and I don't know what."

"What are you doing the rest of the afternoon?"

I had looked forward to going home and napping away my hangover. But I said, "Nothing."

"I found Dr. Vijay Patel. He runs a free clinic in Hollywood."

Surprised, I said, "From the Bel Air Hotel to a free clinic. Are you sure it's the same doctor? Patel is like Smith in India, isn't it?"

"We'll find out."

Over his shoulder, I watched a yellow Maserati pull into the hotel parking lot and stop abruptly. The door flew open. A heavily muscled man unfolded himself from the car, fists clenched. His long dark brown beard couldn't hide his rage.

"Does your client drive a yellow Maserati?"

Heath's head whipped around to the driver's side window "Fuck." He shoved the bag at me. "Hold this."

He was out of the SUV and across the street in seconds, confronting the man. He had a good sixty pounds on Heath and kept trying to walk through him. Heath was talking fast, blocking the man with his body. The man feinted to his left, but Heath stayed with him. Then the man swung his arm. Heath ducked as a big fist breezed narrowly past his head. Catching the man off balance, Heath rose a few inches and jammed his shoulder into him, backing him against his Maserati. Keeping his hands on the man's chest, he talked fast. The man heaved deep breaths. Then Heath, never taking his eyes off him, guided him toward the Escalade.

Opening the back door, he shoved the huge man in.

Heath got behind the steering wheel and locked the doors. "Diana, this is Manfred. Manfred, this is Diana."

"I'm gonna kill you, you son of a bitch," Manfred growled at him.

"Later."

"Where's Rodriquez? He and I get along."

"Dentist. Root canal. I'm taking over for today."

"What's she doing here?" He pointed at me. "Are you screwing her on my time?"

"Not everyone is having sex but you, Manfred."

Manfred mumbled incoherently. His beard was twisted into a braid at the very tip. A diamond barrette held it in place.

Heath let out his breath and checked his watch. "Okay. Roget should be coming out about now. According to Rodriquez, they're like clockwork."

"Fuck." Manfred slumped down in his seat. "It takes her forever with me. I'm so fucking miserable. I gotta hit someone, Heath."

"This doesn't feel right, Manfred. I think you need to sit your wife down and talk to her."

"I wanna kill her."

"It's a refrain," Heath said to me. "Hit. Kill. Kill. Hit."

The hotel door opened, and a beautiful lean blond man strolled out with a canvas bag slung over his shoulder. It was Roget all right.

Manfred shot up. "Tell me it's not him."

"It's him," Heath said, checking the photograph in the file.

He lurched for the door handle. "Open the fucking door."

"Do you want to learn something or not?" Heath snapped.

The blond man sauntered through the parking lot to his car, tossed the canvas bag into the back seat, got in, and drove way.

"What the fuck have I learned?" Manfred exploded. "That she's fucking a fucking Adonis?"

"Relax."

I could hear Manfred breathing heavily behind me. Restless legs bumping. Knuckles cracking.

I turned and gave him a sympathetic smile.

"Hey, I know you. You're Diana Poole," he said, finally focusing.

I nodded. "You love your wife."

"I'll die without her. Or someone will," he added bleakly.

"Here she comes," Heath said. "Right on time."

In no hurry, a tall, voluptuous woman undulated out of the hotel on the highest of heels as if she had been born wearing them. Pausing, she smoothed a tight red dress that showed off her endless legs. If she was trying to hide her assignation, she was doing a terrible job. With silvery hair coiffed, she swayed to the parking lot, and stopped dead when she saw the yellow Maserati.

Spinning around, she faced the black Escalade, threw her head back, red lips spread open, teeth flashing, and let out a long laugh. Then she got into a Mercedes, the same color as her dress, and drove away.

Manfred was thrashing around, pounding on the passenger door window.

"I'm not letting you out," Heath yelled.

"You're fired. Do you hear me? Your name will be shit in this town."

"I'm telling you, Manfred, something else is going on. I've read Rodriquez's report."

"What did she look like when she left the house this morning?" I asked.

The thrashing stopped. His squinty eyes darted to me. "The way she did now."

"Are you sure?" I pursued.

"You think I would forget that dress?"

I turned to Heath. "How did she look when she walked into the hotel?"

He paused, thinking, remembering, then leaned his head back against the seat. "Shit."

"Shit? Shit? What?" Manfred's huge body pressed forward.

"She had her hair pulled back with a rubber band or something." Heath rubbed a hand over his face.

"So what?" Shoving his big head between us, his beard brushed the console.

"She's getting her hair done once a week at the Holiday Inn by Roget," I said.

Eyes slits now, he swung toward Heath. "Does she work for you?"

"No."

"Then what the hell does she know? I'm paying you, not her."

Heath turned sideways, looking at him. His voice was patient. "Think. Once a week like clockwork, according to Rodriquez, the Adonis arrives. An hour and a half later, he comes out with his canvas bag. A few minutes later she shows herself."

"Not with her hair tied back. But done. Coiffed. New hairdo," I added.

"Rodriquez didn't mention that in his report," Heath said to me, his lips forming a sardonic smile.

"You mean he's actually doing her hair in there?" Manfred blew air between his teeth.

"His house calls are very expensive. Must be costing you a fortune," I said.

"I don't understand."

"She wants you to think she's having an affair," Heath said, exasperated. "She wants your attention."

"You mean Ro . . . get is really gay?"

I started to correct him, but Heath shot me a warning look. "Talk to her. Take her out to dinner."

"I'm confused."

"Your wife isn't having an affair. That's all you need to know. Except that you and I are both dumbasses. And Rodriquez is fired."

"You gonna charge me for this?"

Heath unlocked the doors. "What do you think?"

"Why is she having her hair done at the Holiday Inn?"

"Good-bye, Manfred," Heath said. "And don't kill or hit anyone."

Manfred got out of the car and wandered across the street like a man who had lost his sense of purpose.

Heath's amused dark eyes met mine. "I would've sussed it out had it been my case."

"I never doubted you. Will Manfred hurt her?"

"No."

"Are you going to fire Rodriquez?"

He shook his head. "A long talk about his observational skills is all."

He grabbed his phone and punched in a number. "I'm coming in to put something in the safe," he said into the cell. "The Manfred Owen case is closed. Bill him. No, she wasn't screwing around. She was getting her hair done. Is Rodriquez back yet? Okay, tell him to meet me out in front so I won't have to park. Did Madison call? Tell her I'll meet her at La Mer for dinner." He disconnected, took his sunglasses from the dashboard, slipped them on, and started the Escalade's engine.

My hangover pressed down on me. Who the hell was Madison?

# CHAPTER TWENTY

Heath double-parked in front of a one-story brick building on Olympic Boulevard. On the darkened plate glass window was imprinted *HEATH SECURITY*. A man leaned against the front door. Seeing the Escalade, he sauntered toward us. He was wearing a faded black T-shirt, which declared *INKED & EMPLOYED*, and fatigue cargo pants. He smoked a thin cigar. The right side of his cheek puffed out.

Heath rolled down my window and the man leaned in. True to his T-shirt, his arms were tattooed with colorful exotic birds. His black hair waved back from his brown face and shined like an oil slick. A thin, silent movie star–style mustache arched over his upper lip.

"Rodriquez, this is Diana Poole," Heath said.

Blinking through a curl of smoke with dark, crazy eyes, he attempted a sexy smile that ended up in a grimace. "Oh, man, I'm hurting." He put his hand to his swollen cheek.

Heath grabbed the shopping bag. "Put this in the safe. Then go home and go to bed. By the way, Manfred's wife was getting her hair done, not having an affair. You're back behind the computer."

"Oh, man." He looked wounded as he took the bag.

"We're going to talk to Patel, anything I should know?"

"People think he's a saint," Rodriquez said.

I thought of Eddie at StarView telling me Dr. Sam Walford was thought of as a healer to the people he helped.

"Be careful of saints, man." Rodriquez winked at me as he backed away from the car with the small chic shopping bag in his hand.

Heath put up the window and pulled the Escalade into traffic.

"Can he be trusted?" I asked.

"Rodriquez? With my life. He doesn't belong in the field. My mistake. But he's a great detective on the computer."

"Who's Madison?" It was none of my business, but I had to ask.

He looked straight ahead for a few moments, thinking. Then he said, "I needed someone to come in and organize. Keep the billing up to date. She's like an office manager. Things change, Diana."

He was right. It'd been a long time since I'd seen Heath. Things do change. Hell, desire changes. I wondered what Madison looked like. I bet office manager didn't do her justice.

Almost an hour later we were on a side street off Western Avenue. Every house, storefront, or apartment building in the area had some kind of gate or grille to protect the property and lives. Graffiti screamed from walls and sidewalks. Young men and old men lurked in groups as if they'd been bundled and tossed away. There was nothing left to pawn here. Rap music pounded out of cars so loudly you could feel it vibrating inside your body. It wasn't the

Wild West. That was looking forward. This kind of wild was a kid just trying to make it through the night alive.

Heath parked near the free clinic building, which was painted a joyful blue. There was no graffiti on it.

Inside the reception room, toddlers squirmed, cried, and babbled as they waited on their mothers' laps. On the floor, children played with well-used toys. Different languages floated from the kids' mouths. Painted balloons, butterflies, and clouds drifted across sky-blue walls. Children's drawings were taped around the reception window. Some were dedicated to "Dr. Petal" or "Dr. Pedal." In one, a man who was colored Crayola brown wore a white coat and held a big needle. In others, the doctor stood under the sun or a rainbow. In a third, he had a cat sitting on his head. That was my favorite.

"Excuse me," I said to a large ebony-colored woman about the size of Heath. Clad in a smock decorated with tumbling bears, she peered up from her computer. Her full lips were Revlon red.

"We'd like see Dr. Patel," I said.

"Do you have an appointment?" Lips pursed.

"No. If you tell him I'm Diana Poole, Nora Poole's daughter, I think he'd see me."

An unfriendly smile. "That may work where you live, honey, but it don't work here."

Having been taken down a notch, I mumbled, "If you could just tell him I'm here."

Her dark, suspicious eyes roamed over Heath. "And who's he? A cop?"

Heath took out his wallet and showed her his PI license.

She harrumphed. Her large breasts moving up and down with her shoulders. "You still don't have an appointment. Sit down and wait." She watched us as two mothers picked up their kids and put them on their laps, making room for us.

Heath stood. I sat down.

"Thank you," I said. The woman gave me a wan smile then quickly looked away. She knew I was just passing through.

Another woman searched frantically through her battered wallet. Her child tugged her skirt but she took no notice.

I thought of StarView caring for ten patients at thirty thousand dollars a pop.

At the far wall, a door opened. A thin man the color of weak tea wearing a doctor's coat with a stethoscope around his neck came out carrying a small Asian girl in one arm. In his free hand he held a green lollipop. A path of dried tears streaked her face. Her moist lips pouted. Behind them the child's mother neatly folded her daughter's sweater.

Grinning, the doctor swooped the lollypop toward the little girl's mouth. It opened like a baby bird's, and he popped the candy in.

Then he saw me. His smile disappeared. The child forgotten in his arms, he fixed on me as if I were an apparition. Slowly he put the toddler down on the floor, and when he rose up, he'd regained his composure.

He walked toward me. "You gave me a fright. You look so much like your mother. Younger, of course. I'm Dr. Patel." He offered his hand.

I stood and shook it.

"They don't have an appointment," the receptionist growled.

"Thank you, Miss Bell," he said.

"This is Leo Heath." I turned to him and was surprised to see a little boy in his arms playing with his car keys. "We need to talk to you. It won't take long. It's about my mother."

"Yes, yes. Follow me."

"You're running behind now," the receptionist snapped.

"Five minutes."

"It's always five minutes."

Smiling shyly, Heath placed the child in his mother's lap. And I felt a sense of loss. Of family. Never to be. And a deep need to hold onto Heath. Oh, hell.

Dr. Patel led us down a hall past two examining rooms to an office. He sat behind what looked like an old ink-stained teacher's desk. Hanging on the wall behind him were his medical diplomas and more children's drawings.

Heath and I sat in stiff-backed chairs that made me feel as I'd been called into the headmistress's office. Which I had many times. Again I thought of the contrast with StarView. And also the Bel Air Hotel.

"I regret I never got to meet you," Dr. Patel said to me. "It seems our paths never crossed. Your mother spoke frequently of you."

"You were with her often?"

"Yes. I was the hotel doctor. But I also had private patients then. She was under my care. How can I help you?" He spoke precise English with a harmonious lilt. Simple nouns and pronouns sounded important when he said them.

"Do you know Elizabeth Rodgers?" I asked.

"The name is unfamiliar."

"A heavyset woman. Brunette. Probably in her late sixties. She walked into traffic in front of my house. And died. I witnessed her death."

Patel shook his head. "I'm sorry. That must have been a terrible experience for you." Everybody said the same thing.

"You never saw a woman of that description visiting my mother?"

"If she was a friend of your mother's, she never spoke of her. Your mother didn't have many visitors. Ryan Johns, of course. But others could have called on her when I wasn't there."

Heath took out his cell and leaned across the desk, handing it to Patel. When he sat back, the chair squeaked under his weight. "Do you recognize the bracelet?" He'd taken a picture of it yesterday.

Patel held the phone as if it were a Fabergé egg. "No. It's quite unique." He slid the phone across the desk, back to Heath, who pocketed it.

"She kept it on her nightstand. You must've seen it," I said.

"I would have remembered."

"There was an inscription on the inside of the tail of the scorpion," Heath told him. "'To B. Your B.' Do you know what that means?"

His dark eyebrows arched in astonishment. "No."

"You look surprised," I said. "Why?"

"Her name does not begin with a B. Have you asked Ryan Johns about it?"

"Yes. He remembers it on her nightstand. So do I."

"Is it lost? When your mother passed, Ryan Johns was very upset. I do remember I went with him down to the bar and ordered a brandy for him. I was only gone a few minutes. He stayed at the bar."

"Who else was in the room when she died?" Heath asked.

"Only me."

"Paramedics?"

"There was no need."

"Did you call the police?"

"I was her attending physician. The hotel wanted discretion. Is there a problem?"

"No," I said.

Patel looked at me and smiled. "I admired your mother. She and I talked a great deal. She helped me. Told me I was treating the wrong people."

"What did she mean by that?"

"She told me I didn't like my patients, and I couldn't really help people I detested."

"And did you?"

"Not as much as your mother thought, but I didn't respect them. I was a doctor. They treated me like a servant." Bitterness crept into his soft, musical voice. Then he brightened. "She in her own way is responsible for this." He held out his arms, taking in all of his practice.

The door flew wide open. Miss Bell filled its frame. "There are crying children out there, and the ones who aren't have runny noses and fevers. And most of those mothers have buses to catch. Buses that don't wait for them." This was said to me. Turning on her cushioned heel, she marched out, leaving the door open.

Patel raised his hands in surrender and stood. "This clinic would not run if it were not for Miss Bell. I'm afraid she's right. These women are not here on their own time. I'm sorry, I must get back." He took my hand. "Please know your mother loved you in her own way."

"In her own way," I repeated hollowly.

"What other way is there for us to love?" He moved from his desk to the open door.

We walked with him down the corridor.

Heath asked, "Do you know a rehab center called StarView?"

"No." Did he answer too quickly?

"Elizabeth Rodgers was a patient there," I told him. "She had my mother's bracelet with her. I think she wanted to give it me."

"How strange. But then you know where it is? I assumed you were looking for it."

"I'm trying to figure out how it came into her possession."

"I'm sorry I can't be more help."

In the waiting room, Dr. Patel swooped up a screaming little boy and murmured to him. Miss Bell stood behind Patel, hands on her wide hips, glaring at us as we left.

Back in the Escalade, Heath asked me, "Do you think Patel is telling us the whole truth?"

"No."

"Neither do I. He should have seen the scorpion bracelet on her nightstand."

"Yes. I wish he were."

"What?"

"Telling the truth." I stared out the window at this desperate section of the city. Dr. Patel was the one bright, untagged spot of hope. And he'd told me my mother loved me. In her own way.

# CHAPTER TWENTY-ONE

was finally lying down on my bed. Exhausted. My body still reminded me that I was hungover.

Heath had dropped me back at the Holiday Inn to get my car.

I couldn't relax. My mind raced as I went over what I'd learned today. First, "To B. Your B." was engraved on the scorpion. Could be nothing at all. And yet I sensed it had significance. Second, a woman wasn't having an affair with her hairdresser. Great. Third, my mother had helped Dr. Patel find his true calling, but he could have been lying about not seeing the scorpion bracelet.

What else did I know? Heath was having dinner with Madison tonight at La Mer. Too trendy for him. I wondered if this woman was more Madison, Wisconsin, or Madison Avenue.

My cell rang. I grabbed it off the nightstand.

"Hello?"

Silence.

"Did you get the part?"

My body tensed. I sat up. "What?"

"In the movie you read for."

I recognized the voice. "No, Gerard Quincy."

"You found out my name."

"Yes."

"Shit." He sounded panicked. "They're not supposed to give out any information. I have a right to privacy."

"If you mean StarView, they didn't tell me anything."

"Then who did?"

"I have a friend. He found your name."

"What kind of friend?"

"What do you want, Gerard?"

"My gun."

"You know it's not loaded."

"I have bullets."

"Are you in danger?"

"Meet me at eight o'clock tonight at Starbucks, the one in Malibu near Zuma Beach. Good-bye."

"Wait, wait, wait. Before I give you your gun back I want some information."

"At Starbucks."

"Now."

Silence. Only his breathing.

"What do you want to know?"

"You found Elizabeth Rodgers was missing. You got in the Range Rover to go after her. Who was driving it?"

"Not me."

"I know you weren't driving, Gerard."

"I thought we were helping Elizabeth."

"A name."

"Someone she was afraid of. But I didn't know that at the time. I didn't know she would walk into the traffic. Tonight, I'll tell you more."

"Now. Tell me now!"

He hung up.

I opened the drawer and got his gun out.

# CHAPTER TWENTY-TWO

was early. Starbucks was mostly empty except for a woman clinging to her chai frappuccino or whatever it was and her cell phone. A man, eyes so red they looked sunburned, shakily gulped coffee. I brushed a stranger's crumbs from the tabletop and kept my eyes on the entrance. Holding my purse with the gun in it on my lap, I sipped my latte, the warm milk sweet against the sharpness of the coffee. Outside the plate glass window, thick strands of fog curled in the darkness.

Pressing the phone to her chest as if it were something precious, the woman got up and left.

Ten minutes to eight the door opened, and Tanya strode in wearing a black leather jacket, black skintight jeans, and motorcycle boots that looked like they were made for stomping. Tanya had fallen off her lavender yoga mat right into the mean streets without a tremble. She went directly to the counter and ordered. I blinked out the window into the headlights of a limo with its high beams on. Was it waiting for her?

Leaning her elbows on the counter, she stuck out her round, firm ass. The pert ponytail was gone, and her long, silky black hair fanned down her back. The espresso machine roared and gurgled. Hot milk steamed and foamed.

The man with the red eyes got up and walked out, dragging his loneliness with him. He left his cup on the table for someone else to throw away.

Tanya turned; her tilted eyes took in the room then fell on me. Surprise didn't settle well on her face. Her smile grew thin and tough, body rigid.

Composure regained, she swayed over to me. "You're the last person I expected to see."

"Malibu's a small town."

"You here with someone?" Not interested in an answer, her eyes shifted to the waiting limo then back at me.

"Clients?" I asked. "I see you turned in your yoga clothes for a little heavy leather."

"They like me this way." Her dark eyes were defiant. "And listen, Ryan knows what I do." She yelled over her shoulder at the barista. "Hey, hurry it up!"

"You're like a pulp comic book heroine."

"Yeah?" She glanced nervously out the window again.

"Yoga instructor by day. Dominatrix by night. I don't want to see Ryan hurt."

The grinding of the espresso maker stopped.

"I make him happy. Besides, we just met," she said. "We haven't had time to hurt each other."

"It doesn't take a lot of time." I thought of Heath.

The limo suddenly reversed and backed up fast down the parking lot, away from the view of the window.

"Are they leaving without you?"

Agitated, she hurried back to the counter. "I want my coffees now."

The barista made a face as he wedged three drinks into a recycled gray tray and shoved it at her.

"I'll tell Ryan you asked about him," I said, as she picked up the tray and rushed out.

I watched her, haloed in the high beams of the limo as she ran toward it, balancing the drinks. The front passenger door swung open, and soft light spilled from the interior. A large-shouldered, bald-headed man was behind the wheel. The shadowy figures of a blond woman and a man in the backseat embraced. I squinted. Or were they struggling?

Tanya got in next to the driver and pulled the door closed, and the limo sped forward toward me, its lights spreading across my face. Soon it turned toward PCH and floated away in the night fog. I took another sip of my latte. Why had the car backed away from the entrance in the first place? It wasn't blocking anybody. And why was an embrace similar to a struggle? Or was I just projecting my own peculiar view of romance? And who the hell is named Tanya? Not Tanya, I'll bet.

An hour later, the barista began to clean up. "We're closing," he told me, wiping down the counter.

I stood and threw my now empty latte cup into the recycle bin, picked up my purse with Quincy's gun still in it, and walked out into the June gloom. June Gloom. I always thought that sounded like a depressed stripper's name.

# CHAPTER TWENTY-THREE

My front door was ajar. I stared at the wood splintered around the lock and froze. Taking a deep breath, I slowly reached into my purse and took out Quincy's gun. Unloaded gun. I pushed the door open with the tip of my shoe and stepped into my foyer. I paused, listened. My acting skills clicked in. Holding the gun like a real cop, I rushed into the living room.

Sofa cushions were thrown on the floor. The drawers to my side tables hung open. Books and CDs were pulled off the shelves and scattered. Lamps were tipped over. My new chair lay on its pristine side. Even my poor maidenly hydrangea plant had been dumped out of its pot and stomped on. Still in cop mode, I swung into the kitchen. Utensils had been thrown on the floor. Drawers emptied. Refrigerator door hanging open.

I ducked my head into Colin's office. Mother's clothes and clippings were tossed into a pile with Colin's books and scripts. Her Oscar lay stiffly next to his Oscars, small golden corpses among the chaos. A fine gray film of ash blanketed the disarray. Her urn had been dumped over. My cop pose fell apart. I leaned my head against the doorjamb. I should have scattered her ashes long ago.

Turning on my heel, I walked down the hall into my bedroom. It was in the same chaotic condition. Anger flew through me. I rushed back into the kitchen and slammed the refrigerator door shut.

"You little shit!" I yelled, kicking utensils out of my way. A spatula flew.

I threw the gun on the table. How stupid could I be? I kicked at a ladle I'd never used. So Gerard Quincy calls. He's frightened. Wants his gun. Will share information. We set a meeting place. And he doesn't show. Why? Because he's at my house, tearing it apart, looking for the damn scorpion. Shit!

Consoling myself with the fact that the bracelet was safe, I grabbed a glass from the counter, found the Courvoisier bottle in the sink, and poured myself a stiff one. I tossed it back, enjoying the heat and the release. Then I stalked back to the foyer.

There was no way I could lock the front door. I could spend the night at Ryan's, but then I thought of Tanya and decided against it. Grabbing my purse, which I'd dropped on the front porch, I took out my cell and started to call Heath and stopped. He was having dinner with Madison. I played with the idea of going to a motel or hotel for the night, but that would be more depressing than the state of my house.

Shoving the door shut and holding it in place, I managed to put the chain on, the only protection left in one piece. Then I went into the living room and dragged a chest into the foyer and pushed it against the door.

In my bedroom, I hung up the clothes that had been tossed on my bed. I took off my shoes, crawled under the covers, turned on the TV, and took a sleeping pill. Then I took another for good luck.

⌘

"Diana! Diana!"

Hands grabbed me. I flung my arms out.

"Christ, open your eyes."

I did but it was like pulling back the rusty lid of a can of cat food. Heath's face was shoved into mine.

"God, what are you doing here?" I mumbled, trying to push him away.

He let go of me and stood back. "I've been calling you, texting you, all morning. I got worried. What the hell happened here?"

The TV was still on. I sat up, chastely clutching the duvet to my body.

"You've got your clothes on. Besides, I've seen you naked."

"So you have." There was an awkward moment of silence in honor of our naked bodies once pressed together in steamy sex.

Yawning, I brushed my hair out of my face. "Gerard Quincy called. Said he was frightened. Wanted his gun. We decided to meet at Starbucks. He didn't show. I came home to this." I extended my arm, taking in the entire house.

"Christ, you could've been killed."

"What good would that do him or anyone else?"

"It'd stop you from poking around."

"Poking? Is that what you think I'm doing? Is that what you're doing? Poking?"

"All right. All right. You scared the hell out of me." He rubbed his hands through his hair.

"How did you get in?" I yawned again.

"I kicked at the door until the chain broke and the chest moved. And you didn't even hear me crashing and banging around."

106

"I took two sleeping pills so I wouldn't hear such things."

"Good thinking," he said sarcastically. But his face was dark with concern.

"Why were you calling me?"

"Rodriquez wants to talk with you. He's here. He's figured something out."

"Here? What time is it?"

He checked his watch. "Eleven forty-five." He kicked my high heels out of his way and headed toward the door.

"Have a bad time with Madison?" I lowered my lids and tossed him a sexy smile.

He whirled around. "What?"

"I realize I gave you a scare. But you're really grouchy. Like a man who didn't get any last night."

"Get dressed. Or change your clothes or something." He stalked out.

While I quickly put on fresh clothes, brushed my teeth, and combed my hair, I could hear hammering, pounding, and swearing in the foyer. My cell rang. I grabbed it off my nightstand. It was Sheriff Ford asking if I could come to the station around 3:00. I needed to make an identification. He laughed awkwardly and added that it was *nothing gory*. After I told him I would meet him, I hung up, and wondered what nothing gory meant? I checked my voice mail and heard Heath's frustrated calls. Then my agent, who was pissed because he had called yesterday and I hadn't called him back. Now he was pissed again because I wasn't answering and he had a starring role in a Lifetime movie lined up for me. I waited for the hope and excitement of the possibility of a new role. But I didn't feel hope, I didn't feel excited. I didn't call him back. Instead I walked down the hallway to the foyer.

I found Heath had grabbed a piece of wood from my carport and, as Rodriquez held it in place, he hammered it across the door and jamb.

"Good afternoon," Rodriquez said over his shoulder, black hair gleaming like an old Brylcreem ad.

"Same to you. I'll make some coffee."

"It's already made. You might want to get Ryan." Heath reconnected the chain lock he'd broken and the two of them pushed the chest back against the door. I thought about telling them it took just one lone woman to do that last night but decided against it. They looked oddly happy. Even Heath.

I went out the French doors. Ryan and Tanya were running on the hard wet sand along the ocean's edge. Ryan wore tennis shoes. He was falling behind. Tanya, in girly pink sweats, giggled, urging him on. He didn't look right in tennis shoes. He didn't look right running. All arms. All legs. Hawaiian shirt blowing against his beer belly. Face bright red. I missed his Uggs. Who the hell was she? They stopped. He bent over, catching his breath. As I walked down the steps of my deck to the sand, I wondered if she was trying to kill him.

# CHAPTER TWENTY-FOUR

Think of the great lovers." Rodriquez sat next to me at the umbrella table, talking and waving his hand. The tattooed parrots on his arms stared beady-eyed at me. "Tristan and Isolde. Rhett and Scarlett. Jane and Rochester. Pocahontas and John."

"Elizabeth and Darcy, Paris and Helena." Ryan, sitting across from me with a beer in his hand, chimed in. His bright red face had settled down to a calm pink.

Heath leaned against the deck railing, his white shirt bright in the sun. Dark glasses covered his eyes. "Just tell her what you think, Rodriquez."

"What is common about all these names?" he asked.

"They don't begin with the letter *B*," I said.

"No. No. Let's take Jane and Rochester. Let's say he gave her the scorpion bracelet. Let's say he wanted to engrave only their initials on it because, well, he does have a wife. It'd read: 'To J. Yours R.' The engraving on the scorpion reads 'To B. Your B.' Now if Rochester had put it that way it'd mean To Jane your Rochester. Which of course she isn't. She's Jane."

"Rodriquez," Heath warned him.

"Process is important," Ryan said to Heath.

Rodriquez grinned at Ryan. A man after his own heart. Heath turned restlessly and looked out at the ocean. I watched his tense broad back. He was a man of action, not process.

My phone buzzed and danced on the table. Heath turned back, and all three men stared at it.

"Aren't you going to answer?" Heath asked.

I glanced at the screen. "No." It was my agent again.

Ryan drew my phone to him. "It's your agent," he said, concerned.

Not returning your agent's phone call in Hollywood was suicidal. What was I flirting with?

"Go on, Rodriquez." I nodded at him.

"There is one more pair of lovers. But they do not have normal names. In fact one of them isn't normal at all."

"To Beauty. Your Beast," I said. "Of course."

"*Olé.*" He leaned back in his chair with a satisfied grin. "Now all you have to do is find a man who looks like a beast."

"You don't have to look like a beast to be one," I said.

A grin slipped across Heath's face.

I shifted my gaze to Ryan. "Did my mother ever mention having a man who was her beast?"

"No. But she loved telling the story about Greta Garbo watching the movie directed by Cocteau."

"What story?" Heath asked.

"Jean Cocteau was a French director who made *Beauty and the Beast* into in a film," I said. "He was showing it at a private screening. Garbo was there. At the end of the movie when the beast turned into a prince and before the lights came up, the guests heard Garbo's deep Germanic voice saying, 'I *vant* my beast back.' My mother loved that story."

"Why?" Heath asked.

"The longing for what was real. The beast. Not the prince," I said.

"You think your mother found him?" Heath asked.

"I don't know. Ryan?"

"Sorry." He shook his head.

"Dr. Patel said he never saw the scorpion bracelet," I told him.

"She always had it on her nightstand." He swallowed some beer.

"Maybe she put it away when he was there. Maybe she didn't want him to see it." Heath sat down at the table. I felt his knee brush against mine. He quickly moved it away.

"But why?" Ryan asked him.

"I hate this business." Rodriquez's parrots looked as if they were going to fly off his arms. "We solve one clue and feel so *victorioso*. Then there are a hundred more questions to answer. And we are *idiotas* again."

"You did great," I said.

"I'm hot. I'm going swimming." Ryan stood.

"You don't know how to swim," I said, surprised.

"Tanya's teaching me."

As if on cue she came out of Ryan's house onto his verandah wearing a bikini the color of the sun. Her firm latte-hued body glowed from the reflection of her swimsuit.

Rodriquez leaped to his feet and bowed to her. Then he turned to Ryan and clapped him on his back. "So you are a *bestia*."

Ryan laughed as Tanya tossed her hair, and before I could tell him not to say anything to her about our conversation, he was bolting down the stairs and up his.

As they disappeared inside his house, I said, "I saw her last night at Starbucks while I was waiting for Gerard Quincy."

"What was she doing?" Heath turned to me, alert.

"She was in a limo. Her clients were in the backseat. She came in to get coffee for them. She was dressed in black jeans, leather jacket, motorcycle boots. The odd thing was the limo had moved away from the front of Starbucks."

"Why?" Rodriquez asked.

"It was as if the people inside didn't want to be seen. Do hookers get coffee?"

Heath and Rodriquez looked sheepishly each other, then peered back at me and shrugged in unison.

"Check her out," Heath told Rodriquez.

"A pleasure."

"On the computer," Heath reminded.

"My life is so narrow. Does she have a last name?"

"I don't know," I said.

"That can't be her real name," Heath said to Rodriquez.

"True. Now my life is more exciting."

"I've got to meet Sheriff Ford." I stood.

The two men got to their feet.

"I'll get you a new front door," Heath said.

"I'll take care of it."

"I don't want to have to worry about you." He sounded exasperated, which annoyed me.

Sensing an argument, Rodriquez bounced lightly down the deck steps to the pathway by the side of my house.

"You don't *have* to do anything, Heath."

He studied me through his dark glasses."Let me know what Ford has to say. And lock the French doors when you leave."

"Maybe it would be easier for both of us if we just went to bed. Together."

"Get it over with?"

"Break the tension. Yes. Get it out of the way."

He rubbed the bump on his nose as Rodriquez slunk around the corner of the house. "We've done that already."

I went inside, closed the French doors, and locked them.

# CHAPTER TWENTY-FIVE

The Malibu Sheriff's station wasn't in Malibu, it was in Lost Hills, which wasn't lost. Like other buildings in the area, it had a forced modern appearance of the now, which made it look passé. The portico was designed with huge muscle-bound pillars holding up a giant slab of white cement over glass doors that were as dark as a rapper's car windows.

I got out of the Jag. The valley heat had sucked up all the June gloom mist. The air was as clear as a bell.

Inside, the station master walked me down a brightly lit hallway to Ford's office. I didn't see any people in handcuffs waiting for the axe to fall, or harried detectives complaining about paperwork, or prostitutes being hassled by big-bellied cops. Maybe there was a separate entrance for the lost of Lost Hills and Malibu.

The station master stopped abruptly and knocked firmly on a door with a big dangerous-looking fist. It should have been smeared with a perp's blood, but instead it was stained with bureaucratic ink. It's possible I'd been in too many TV shows where cops kick down doors and bend the rules. Yet this sanitized station was more sinister to me than anything Hollywood could come up with.

Deputy Sheriff Ford barked, "Come in."

Ford, sitting at his desk, got quickly to his feet, as did Marc Decker.

"Ms. Poole, good of you to come," Ford greeted.

The station master withdrew with the air of a well-trained butler.

Ford continued, "I believe you know Mr. Decker."

"Yes." My defenses shot up. I wasn't familiar with police protocol, but I didn't like having the head of StarView here without being warned or asked my permission.

I looked at Decker. "I thought you were in Mendocino, making plans for a new rehab center."

"I was called back," he said evenly.

"Since you've already talked with Marc," Deputy Sheriff Ford said, "I didn't think you'd mind if he joined us."

"We have the same concerns," Decker added.

Noting they were on a first-name basis, I decided not to tell him that I doubted we had the same concerns.

"Why don't we all sit down?" Ford gestured toward a chair. "How was the traffic?" He settled into his big leather desk chair.

"Awful. I hope I didn't keep you waiting too long." I glanced at Decker while sitting down.

"No, no." He was elegant in another expensive suit. Long legs crossed. No glimpse of skin between the top of his socks and the hem of his trousers. That would be inelegant.

"Last time I talked to you, you were up for a role in a movie. How did it go?" Ford asked.

"I didn't get the part."

"I don't know how you actors do it. Well, I won't keep you any longer than I have to." Ford was doing his obsequious act.

He took a zip-lock plastic bag out of his drawer and slid it across his desk to me. "Is this a photo of the man who held you at gunpoint?"

I stared at Gerard Quincy's picture on his driver's license. "Yes, that's the same man."

Decker let out a disappointed sigh. "I was hoping it wasn't. I just can't believe Gerard would attack you with a gun. What reason would he have?"

"Why don't you ask him?" I looked at Ford.

"I'm afraid he's dead," Ford said.

"Oh. How did he die?"

"From what we can tell, it looks as if he shot himself. A suicide or an accident." Ford leaned back, resting his hands on his belly. "He was found in the Malibu RV Park. He'd been hiding out there in a trailer ever since he ran away from StarView. A couple in a nearby camper thought they heard a backfire around seven thirty last night. Didn't think much about it. Later when they went outside to have a cigarette and some beers they noticed his door was open. They went to check. Found his body."

"Then they immediately called you?" I asked.

"Yes. Of course there's always the question of whether it was a gunshot they heard and not a backfire. The coroner will have a more definite time when he's finished with his examination."

I felt hollow inside. If Gerard Quincy died around that time, then that's why he didn't show up at Starbucks. That's why he couldn't be the intruder who'd ransacked my house. I kept my voice steady. "And he shot himself with what?"

Ford brows knitted. "His gun."

Decker leaned toward me. "This must be a shock for you. I know it is for me. Gerard was a good man. Not being able to save Elizabeth Rodgers had to be unbearable for him."

"He shot himself with his own gun," I repeated, ignoring Decker. I thought of his weapon in my nightstand drawer. I thought of him asking for it. I thought of these two men sitting here all buddy-buddy.

"Yes." Ford frowned.

"Do you have the gun?" I asked.

Ford opened his desk drawer and came out with a gun in a plastic bag and pushed it toward me.

I peered at it. "A Glock."

"You know your weapons." Ford sounded like a proud father.

Decker shifted in his chair, adjusting his jacket.

"Not really. Directors love to use Glocks in their movies."

Ford's big hand swept the plastic bag back into his drawer. "So I think we have what we need. You've identified Gerard Quincy and his weapon. I want to thank you for coming in." He stood. "And I'm sorry you had to go through all this."

I remained seated. "Oh, I didn't identify Quincy's gun." I gestured toward the desk drawer. "I merely said that was a Glock."

"What?" Confused, Ford shifted his weight.

"Gerard's weapon wasn't that make. The one he held on me was a Smith and Wesson. And Quincy didn't strike me as the kind of guy who'd have two guns. He had trouble enough with one. You know, he phoned me yesterday."

Decker's eyes were hooded, and he was smoothing his tie as if it had come alive and he had to tame it.

Ford eased himself carefully back into his chair. "What did he want?"

"He was afraid for his life." I turned to Decker. "Afraid the person driving the StarView Range Rover was going to harm him."

"We've been through that, Ms. Poole. I checked. Eddie, our security man, didn't see another person get into that car with Quincy." He turned to Ford. "He keeps tabs on our Rovers."

I crossed my legs. "I only know what Quincy told me."

"What time did he call you?" Ford suddenly appeared haggard under his tan.

"Around five thirty. He wanted to meet me at Starbucks at eight. I was hoping he could tell me about Elizabeth Rodgers and how she came to have my mother's bracelet. But of course, he didn't show."

"What bracelet?"

"It has a scorpion charm on it. My mother's birth sign. I found it in the debris of the accident. I showed it to Decker. I'm surprised he didn't tell you about it." I never looked at Decker.

Ford swung his head toward him. "You never mentioned anything about a scorpion bracelet."

"I didn't think it was important." Decker shrugged it off.

Lips pursed, Ford studied me. When he spoke, it was obvious he was trying to control his temper. "You should've come to me first, Ms. Poole. Are you keeping anything else from me?"

I paused. Waited. Then I said, "I have Quincy's gun."

"You what?" His blond brows arched. A vein throbbed in his right temple.

Decker's lips pressed together.

"He left it on my front porch the night he held me up," I explained. "It wasn't loaded. He said he wanted me to bring it to Starbucks because he needed it. He was afraid for his life."

Ford slammed his hands on his desk and shot to his feet. "I may do my best to protect the reputations of the people in my community, but nobody's above the law, including you, Ms. Poole!"

"I don't like being set up, Sheriff." I scrambled to my feet. Decker was staring at something on the ceiling. "I don't like Decker sitting in on our meeting. And I don't like the death of a poor helpful idiot like Quincy being swept under the rug so you can appease StarView." Grabbing my purse, I pulled open the door and walked down the hall toward the front portico, expecting someone to stop me. But no one did.

# CHAPTER TWENTY-SIX

My adrenaline was pumping as I drove away from the sheriff's station and back into Malibu. If Gerard Quincy was already dead when I was waiting for him at Starbucks, then who the hell broke into my house?

Pulling into my carport, I saw a group of men working on my front door. As I got out of my car, Rodriquez hurried toward me.

"Do you remember Manfred?" he asked.

"You mean hit-kill-kill-hit Manfred? I'll never forget him. What's going on?"

"Well, he wanted to get you something for solving his case and bringing him and his lady back together."

"And?"

"Manfred thought jewelry. I agreed with him," Rodriquez said, nervously smoothing his thin-line mustache. "But Heath mentioned you needed a new front door, and he gave him the measurements. Now because a man has money doesn't mean he has taste."

"Manfred bought me a front door?" With Rodriquez right behind me, I marched out of the carport around to the front of my house and down the brick path and stopped.

Two men who looked like thugs were packing up their carpentry tools. One had a scar that ran from his ear to the corner of his mouth. Manfred's bald head shined with sweat. The diamond barrette twinkled at the braided tip of his long beard. Huge hands on huge hips, he stood legs apart, proudly surveying his gift.

I gaped at a teak door. Two dolphins, looking as if they had just leaped straight up from the ocean, were carved in relief and ran the entire length of the door. Their snouts, or whatever dolphins have, jutted so far from the door I could have hung a hat on each one. They greeted me with beady eyes and supercilious grins. Between them was a carved garish yellow sun.

"Hey, here she is. The woman who saved my marriage. Something Rodriquez and Heath couldn't do. This is for you!" Manfred gestured expansively toward the door. "What do think? I knew you lived in Malibu, so I wanted to keep a beachy feel going." He flashed big square teeth at me.

"I'm . . . I'm . . . astonished."

"Hey, get these things out of her way and go wait in the car," he ordered the thugs, who took their tools and trudged off. "Nobody's ever breaking in this door. Feel the thickness." He pounded on it. *Thump. Thump.* "Open it, feel the weight."

I took hold of the large iron handle, turned, and pushed. Nothing. Finally I threw my shoulder into it and shoved. The door flew open, taking me with it. I shot Rodriquez a look. He lingered on the porch, his hands held out, helpless.

In the foyer, Manfred closed the door and showed me its back-side. It, too, was carved. Fish and sexy mermaids, thank God not in relief, swam through wavy seaweed. The bilious yellow sun was bright above them.

"Dig this." He slid the sun to one side. "You can look out, but nobody can see in. One-way bulletproof glass. Heath wanted you to be safe. And you are." He beamed. I peered through the glass and watched Rodriquez petting one of the dolphins.

"I'm speechless. Where did you get it?"

"Don't ask. But just between us, it's a forty-thousand-dollar door."

"Forty . . . I couldn't possibly let you spend . . ."

"That's retail. I don't buy nothing retail." He took my hand in his big paw, turned it over, and kissed my palm. I felt more beard than lips. "My wife and me thank you."

I gave up. "Thank you, Manfred."

He opened the door as if it were light as a Kleenex and strode outside. "You coming, Rodriquez?" He moved toward a white con-vertible Bentley where the two thugs sat in back looking at their phones.

"Manfred picked me up at the office," Rodriquez explained. A car revved loudly. It wasn't the Bentley.

I followed Rodriquez's gaze across PCH to a black Porsche, tires squealing, as it pulled away from the embankment into traffic. Hell, it was Peter Bianchi. How long had he been there?

Rodriquez's eyes were now on me, studying me. For the first time, they weren't dancing. They were unnervingly steady.

Without missing a beat, he said, "Heath's coming by later to check the door. The dolphins kinda grow on you. Adios, *belleza.*" Moving like a ballroom dancer, he glided to the car where Manfred and his guys waited.

# CHAPTER TWENTY-SEVEN

had my bedroom picked up and was starting on the living room by the time Heath arrived. He did the impossible. He ignored the dolphins on the front door. Now he stood out on the deck, his hands gripping the railing in silent anger, staring out at the darkening misty sky and ocean. He hadn't even asked me about my meeting with Sheriff Ford.

The problem with silent anger is that it's incredibly loud and exasperating. And it permeates. I snatched up a box of matches from the floor near the fireplace and walked out to where he stood. I struck a match and lit the hurricane candle, watching it dance to life.

Then I tossed the box on the table and said, "Okay, Heath. Do you want to tell me what's going on? Because if you don't, then you should leave. I have a house to clean up. And you're annoying me."

He turned around. Eyes hooded, shadows from the candlelight jumped across his face. "When were you going to tell me?"

"Tell you what?"

"That Peter Bianchi is stalking you."

I took a deep breath. "I wouldn't call it stalking."

"Really?" His fingers clasped and unclasped. "Rodriquez said Bianchi sat in his Porsche and stared at the house and the guys putting up the front door for a good half hour. Then you arrived, and he made a big deal about revving his engine, spinning his tires, and speeding off so everyone, especially you, would see him. Now why do you think he did that? Because he's not stalking you?"

"It's only been a few days since we broke up. How did you know it was him?"

"Rodriquez got his plate number, called me, and I got someone to run it for me."

"I don't think Peter's ever been rejected before."

"So he'll get over it? Christ, Diana, you sound like the woman who goes to the ER with a broken nose and two black eyes and says her husband didn't mean it and won't do it again."

"I'm not a victim, Heath."

"No. Diana Poole's invincible." He pushed away from the railing, shoved his hands in his jeans pockets, and paced the length of the deck. "Tell me the story again about how you just happened to have flowers and then a sudden urge to run across PCH and place them on the debris of the accident. How did you even know there was debris there?"

"All right." I slammed my hand on the table. "Peter left the flowers on top of the L.A. Times. I saw he was parked on the embankment. It made me furious. So without thinking I ran across the highway to confront him."

"What happened?"

"I couldn't stop swearing at him and he compared me to a beach town that looks old and shabby in the daylight. Then he drove off."

"And he's back today. But he's not stalking you."

"What do you want me to say, Heath?"

He stopped moving and faced me. "I want you to think like a normal person."

"What the hell does that mean?"

"It means that you can't fix or control an ex-lover from stalking you. It means you have to protect yourself."

"I am a normal person."

"Like hell you are." He strode back into the living room and kicked a sofa cushion. It arced high in the air and came down on top of my new chair. Then he headed for the front door.

I followed him. "That's it? You come here and criticize me for being stalked, as if it's my fault, and now you're leaving?"

"I came here to make you see the reality of what Peter Bianchi is doing."

"Mission accomplished. What about the case we're working on?"

"What about it?"

"Don't you want to hear about my meeting with Ford?"

"I heard through the grapevine that Quincy committed suicide."

"You don't believe that, do you?"

"No." He opened the door. The simpering dolphins swung into view.

"That means it wasn't Quincy who ransacked my house. It has to be someone from StarView. Damn it, where are you going, Heath?"

"I'm having dinner with Madison. She wants to try a new restaurant called Nouveau."

"You're joking."

"No. I'm not. Now would you please lock this goddamn piss-ugly door?" He slammed it shut behind him.

My house shook so violently I thought it was going to fall down around me.

After shoving the bolt in place, I went to the kitchen and opened the refrigerator. I pulled out a cold half-empty bottle of Pinot Noir, took a glass off the counter, and poured myself some.

I took a gulp and leaned against the counter. Christ.

And then I felt a biting cold creep through me. An icy intruder in my very soul.

Maybe it wasn't someone from StarView who did this to my house. Maybe it wasn't anyone connected to the case. Maybe it was a disturbed ex-lover. Maybe it was Peter Bianchi.

# CHAPTER TWENTY-EIGHT

P eter Bianchi lived high in the hills off of Sunset Plaza Drive. In my Jag, I curved around the steep road until I swung a right on Sparrow Place. I slowed and parked near Peter's security gate, dimly lit by solar lights.

Heath was right. I'm not a normal person. When I realized Bianchi might be the one who had ransacked my house, I just leaped into my car and drove here. Surprise is always a good advantage, but I have to admit that didn't occur to me until now. Anger is a great motivator. And I was thriving on it.

I got out of my car. I knew Bianchi's security code. Ex-lovers know these things. I punched in his number on the pad and waited for the gate to slide sideways across the fern-lined driveway. I followed it up to the front door of his retro modern house. The porch light was on. The door was ajar. I paused. How many slightly open doors can one woman encounter in two days? The wood wasn't splintered. The lock wasn't broken.

I took a deep breath and slipped inside as quiet as a piece of silk. In the hall landing gold-streaked mirrors reflected my lurking image over and over. A small crystal chandelier glittered above me. I heard a gasping sound and stepped toward the living room and stopped dead.

"Heath!" I ran into the room.

Heath's broad back was to me. His left hand was around Bianchi's throat shoving him up against the view window. He had his right arm pulled back, ready to slam his fist into Bianchi.

"Stop it!" I grabbed at his arm. He jerked free. He still had a hold on Bianchi's throat. Heath had that look on his face as if he didn't know me. Bianchi was wide-eyed, lip split, ashen with fear.

"Let go of him, for Christ's sake." I gripped his arm again, trying to pull him away from Bianchi.

Heath let go of Bianchi's throat. Bianchi slid to the floor, legs and arms akimbo. The full vista of the glittering Los Angeles basin came into sight.

"What the hell are you doing?" Furious, I turned on Heath.

"Making sure he won't stalk you again." Heath spoke in a matter-of-fact voice. "What are you doing?"

I kneeled next to Bianchi. "Is he alive?"

"Fuck you," Bianchi said to me.

Heath moved to the leather-tufted retro bar and leaned against it. "I know how to hurt people, Diana, without killing them."

Bianchi moaned, grimaced, and gingerly sat up, slumping back against the window.

"He's got an actor's body. All show." Heath took a cocktail napkin with Peter's name printed on it in gold from a stack on the bar. He dabbed at the knuckles on his right hand.

I glared at him. "Did you bother to ask him if he broke into my house?"

"He didn't break in. But he did see someone."

I looked at Bianchi. "Who?"

"You." Bianchi managed a slight grin.

"Me? What the hell are you talking about?" I looked at Heath. "He's lying."

"I don't think so," Heath said.

Bianchi wiped spittle from his lips and his bruised eyes met mine. "I saw you and some big guy going into the house."

"It was foggy last night. Did you see my face?"

"Just your back, blond hair."

Confused, I looked at Heath again. He just raised his eyebrows at me, then balled the cocktail napkin up and put it in his jacket pocket. "What time did you see this?" he asked.

"I don't know. Sometime after eight o'clock."

"What did the man look like? Was he the size of Heath? Bigger? Smaller?"

"Chunkier, shorter. Didn't see his face. I drove away. Now get the hell out of my house. I have an early call tomorrow."

"Early call? God, I hope makeup can cover your black eyes," I said wryly.

He reached up to his face. "Fuck you. Fuck you both."

I leaned down. "Don't ever come near me again. Do we understand each other?" He turned his head away.

I rose up and headed to the front door. Heath was right behind me.

Outside, I breathed in air. "How the hell did Peter ever let you in?" I snapped.

"I climbed over the gate, knocked on the door. He answered. And the rest you can imagine."

"Well, I don't want to." I was just as angry with Heath as I was with Bianchi.

We began to walk down the driveway.

"So who's the other blonde?" he asked.

"I have no idea. What about the man he saw? It could still be someone from StarView, or maybe Dr. Patel?"

"Patel is the wrong body type. So is Decker, the shrink Walford, even Eddie."

"Now we have a blonde and a man we don't know. Perfect." We stopped at the gate. "Did you just decide to go beat up Bianchi instead of dine at Nouveau?"

Puzzled, his brows knitted. "Oh. The restaurant. Yes. I had to cancel. Madison and I are going tomorrow night."

Shaking my head, I jabbed in the code again, and it slid slowly to one side.

"You know the code," Heath said.

"Yes."

"Of course you would."

"Of course," I echoed his dry tone.

We continued to walk. The gate closed behind us.

"How do we even know Bianchi's telling the truth?" I asked.

"It's one thing to stalk a woman. It's another thing to take a beating for it. I think he told us what he saw. What do you think? You're the one who had an affair with him."

At the bottom the drive I stopped and confronted him. "What the hell does that mean?"

He shrugged. "It means you know him better than I do."

"No, it doesn't. There was an accusation in that statement."

"Let's forget it."

"I will not. Let me remind you of something. The last time we saw each other you asked me if I wanted to see you again. You didn't wait for my answer. You turned away from me. Disappeared from my life. Before I had an affair with Bianchi. Why did you do that? Were you afraid I might have said yes?"

He bent his head, his somber eyes on me. "I'll tell you what the problem is, Diana. It's not that you had an affair with a jerk like

Bianchi. That's your choice. It's when you came into his house just now and yelled for me to stop. I saw your expression. You weren't frightened. Oh no, not you. But you were disgusted. Repulsed by my methods. I'm not an actor. I'm the real thing. We would never stick. That's why I didn't wait for your answer. That's why I walked away." He turned and strode down the street. I watched him disappear into the shadows.

"That's bullshit, Heath!" I shouted after him. My voice ricocheted around the dark, quiet neighborhood. I got into my car and sped away.

# CHAPTER TWENTY-NINE

There's always another blonde. But who was this one?

It was the next afternoon. I sat on my deck waiting for Deputy Sheriff Ford to come and pick up Quincy's gun, which I still had in my nightstand.

The fog had dissipated early; the sun was out and warm. More people were walking their dogs. I watched the same two older women strolling along, chattering away, stopping, laughing. Their bond of friendship and shared-time was palpable. A sharp pain of melancholy twisted through me. I had somehow lost the knack for developing friends. Except for Ryan.

Leaning back on my lounge, I closed my eyes against the sun and let my mind drift with the repetitive sound of the surf. Soon

I was dozing, a luxurious feeling I hadn't allowed myself in a long time.

"You got any beer?"

At the sound of Tanya's voice, I shot upright, eyes opened. She loomed in front of me. I blinked. A flash of red shimmered around her, then faded as my eyes adjusted to the brightness. She was back in her Lululemons and acting as if she had all her chakras perfectly aligned. The tough, leather-souled woman I met in Starbucks was gone.

"Ryan wants one and I don't feel like going to the market. He's writing about zombies." She tossed her long, black shiny mane. "They exist, you know."

I squinted at her. "Who exists?"

"Zombies. They're called working zombies—you give them this white powder. It seeps through their skin and makes them do what you want. I told Ryan about it. He's doing the research. You see? I'm good for him."

I let out a sigh. "What exactly was it you wanted?"

"Beer."

I got up, and we walked into the kitchen, which I hadn't picked up yet.

Surprised by the mess, she blurted, "Shit, that was some bad recipe you were trying. So what happened here?"

"My house was broken into." Leaning against the refrigerator, I watched her.

"Wow. Just the kitchen?" She peered around.

"No, the entire house."

"Did they take anything?" She tucked her hair behind her ear.

"No."

"That's weird."

"What they were looking for wasn't here."

"Lucky you, I guess." She nudged an eggbeater with her bare foot. "Who uses this thing anymore?"

Ignoring her question, I asked, "Don't you want to know what my intruders were looking for?" I tried to imagine her in a blond wig.

Her almond-shaped eyes slid sideways to mine. Her face lost its curiosity. "What about that beer?"

I turned and opened the refrigerator. "When I saw you at Starbucks there was a couple in the back seat of the limo. Who were they?" I took out two bottles and pushed the door shut with my hip.

"My clients. And I never give out names. It's bad for business."

"The woman was a blonde."

"So?"

"Somebody saw a blond woman and a man break into my house."

"Trust me, it wasn't her."

"But I don't trust you." I handed her the beers.

She held one in each hand. "You're not like Ryan. He always gives a person a chance."

"He wants your body."

She smiled seductively. "Now you're not giving *him* a chance."

"Where did you go after you left Starbucks?" Crossing my arms, I rested against the counter.

"To their house."

"With coffee?"

"They hate booze. Love sex."

"Why did the limo back away from the entrance so quickly? It was almost as if the couple in the rear didn't want to be seen by me."

"Famous people sometimes don't want to be recognized. Why all the questions?" Tilting her head caused her long silky hair to cascade to one side, creating a dark shadow over the side of her face.

"I'm trying to figure out who you really are. When I first saw you, you used the word 'serendipity' to describe your encounter with Ryan."

"So?"

"You should've used the word 'karma.' It would've fit better with the yoga part you're playing. And in Starbucks you seemed more like a gofer than a high-paid call girl."

Her body straightened. Lips pursed, she stared at the beer in her right hand. Then she shoved her thumb under the edge of the bottle cap and flipped it off. It arced into the sink next to me. She took a long swallow and walked out of my house.

After a moment, I opened the refrigerator and took out a beer and placed the tip of my thumb under the cap and pressed upward. The sharp corrugated edge dug hard into my flesh. I put the bottle back and rubbed the pain out of my thumb.

Soon I began picking up cutlery, bowls, pans. Many of them I never used. Colin, my husband, had done all the cooking, or we ate out. I stuffed everything into the dishwasher. I put in detergent that made dishes sparkle and turned the thing on. It murmured contently like a well-fed animal.

The doorbell rang, sending a kind of anxiety through my house. I wiped my hands on the back of my jeans and went to peer out my window.

Deputy Sheriff Ford scrutinized the dolphins as if he was going to arrest them. I opened up.

"This is some door," he said, stepping inside.

"Yes it is." I shoved it closed.

"Looks expensive."

"It was."

"I'm always amazed at how much actors make." There was something in his voice. Jealousy? Was he resentful of the rich and famous he protected on a bureaucrat's salary?

"Well?" He was staring at me. Waiting.

"I'll get the gun."

"I'll get it. It's not just a gun anymore, it's evidence. Where is it?"

"This way." He followed me down the hall into my bedroom, and I pointed at the drawer in my nightstand. "In there."

Ford took a pair of gloves from his pants pocket and put them on. They made him look menacing, as if he didn't want to leave his fingerprints in my house, let alone on the weapon.

He opened the drawer, reached in, and came out with two bottles of sleeping pills. "I hope you're careful with these."

"I am."

"I've seen a few people who've OD'd unintentionally." He put them back.

I shifted uneasily.

Then he took an evidence bag from his jacket pocket, removed the gun from the drawer, and without looking at it, slid it into the evidence bag.

"It's not loaded," I told him. "It hasn't been fired."

"Forensics will tell us what we need to know. You shouldn't have kept this."

"It wasn't intentional."

He gave me a long, hard look. His tanned skin was blotchy, and the veins on his nose were broken, spreading little bloody trails onto his cheeks. He looked like he'd been drinking. He was making me uncomfortable standing in my bedroom with his protective gloves on.

"You're not keeping anything else from me, are you?" he asked.

"No." I started back down the hall. I could hear him behind me. I quickly opened the front door.

He stopped. His expression told me he had no intention of leaving.

"I'm busy, Sheriff."

"*Deputy* Sheriff." He placed the evidence bag on the small hall table and began to methodically remove his gloves. "Do you know a woman who calls herself Tanya?"

"Why?" I kept my voice even.

"It's a simple yes or no question." He bunched the gloves up and stuffed them into his pants pocket.

"I've seen her on the beach."

"Many residents don't know this, but prostitutes troll our beautiful beaches looking for rich men and women. A few of those men and women have been robbed. You might want to tell your friend Ryan Johns to be very careful."

"How did you know about her and Ryan?"

"I'm a cop. And I don't like whores on my beach. Do you?" His washed-out eyes challenged me. There was hatred behind that word *whore*. I could feel it.

I didn't answer.

"She's dangerous."

"Why don't you arrest her?"

"I'm the law. I need a reason." He picked up the evidence bag and walked out.

Standing in the doorway, I rested my hand on the dolphin's needle nose. It was warm from the sun. I watched Ford stalk to his patrol car, get in, and drive away. There was no doubt he had his own agenda, and that it included Marc Decker. So why was he warning me about Tanya? Because he didn't like whores? No. There was something else. And he never mentioned wanting to see the scorpion bracelet. That's what had started this whole mess. Why wasn't that evidence?

Ryan loped into view along PCH.

"Where are you going?" I called out.

Pausing, he glanced toward me. "Walking. Need to think. May go to Kiki's for a bite."

"Why not walk on the beach?"

"I need lots of car exhaust to think. Tanya's given me this great idea . . ." He stopped. His head jutted forward, eyes childlike as he rushed toward me.

Pointing at the dolphins, he cried, "Flipper. Two Flippers!"

"Who is Flipper?"

# CHAPTER THIRTY

Y ou don't know who Flipper is?" Ryan gaped at me as if I didn't recognize the name "Einstein." His curly red hair was rumpled. So was his Hawaiian shirt.

We were still standing by my open front door.

"No, I don't."

"Ranger Porter Ricks, Sandy, Bud, and their pet dolphin, Flipper. They were a family."

Now I gaped at him.

"A TV series in the early sixties," he explained.

"You weren't even born then."

"You of all people should know about reruns." He perused the door. "This looks like something I'd choose, not you. You have taste."

"It wasn't my choice. I need to talk to you. It's important."

"If it's about Tanya . . ."

"How much have you told her about what Heath and I are looking into?"

"Not much. She thinks I should call Heath off. But I told her there was no way of calling you off."

"Why does she think you should stop the investigation?"

"Because I'm writing now, and she doesn't want anything to upset my flow. She's good for me."

"That's what she told me."

"It's true. I've been working all day."

I looked down at the floor, debating whether I should tell him what Ford had said. Of course I wasn't sure whether I trusted Ford any more than I trusted Tanya. But if something happened to Ryan, and I hadn't warned him . . .

Glancing up at him, I said, "Deputy Sheriff Ford was just here to pick up Quincy's gun. He said Tanya was dangerous." I left out the part about her being a whore. "If he was aware of her, that means she has a record or had a run-in with the police. Or maybe harmed someone."

All warmth and humor drained from his face. "She's not dangerous."

"How do you know that? She pops up out of the sand the day after the accident. It's like she was waiting there for you. As if she was put there by . . ."

"By whom? Who put her there? Can you hear how ridiculous you sound? If you value our friendship, then I don't want to hear any more about what you think or somebody else thinks about Tanya. I'm writing because of her." He threw his hands up in the air. "About zombies for fuck's sake!" He turned and walked away.

I closed the door and leaned my head against the yellow sun. Soon my brain began to work. I tugged open the door and ran after Ryan, who was slumping down PCH.

"Wait!" I caught up with him.

He stopped and glared at me, red lashes glittering in the sunlight. Cars sped by us.

"Do you know a blonde?" I asked.

"You mean besides you?"

"Yes."

"Is she dangerous?"

"She might be. Looks like me from the back."

"Turn around."

I did.

"Gabrielle Hays."

Stunned, I faced him. "Why her?"

"Because you both have fat asses and no shoulders. And droopy ankles."

I made a face.

"All right, all right. She's the first name that came to me. You're a little taller, but you have similar figures and similar hair length. And you refer to her as your blond shadow."

"I do, don't I?" I threw my arms around him. "Ryan. I worry about you . . ."

He stepped back from me. "Don't start."

"I'm not. But . . ."

"Enough, Diana."

As I watched him continue on his way to Kiki's, I thought of Gabrielle Hays. My nemesis. My blond shadow. My doppelgänger. Gabrielle who got the part I wanted. Gabrielle who paused on the stairwell and asked me about the accident. Gabrielle who had dark circles under her eyes, whose lips quivered when she spoke. Gabrielle who had never stopped to speak to me before.

I walked back to my house. In the living room, I paced the length of it. Yes, Gabrielle never spoke to me unless she absolutely had to. But she did the day after the accident. What had she said?

Something about she'd heard it had happened in front of my house. How did she know that? How did she know where my home was exactly?

My mother once said that an actress should never pace in a scene. It's an action the untalented choose. And please don't wring your hands. Have you ever seen anyone wring their hands? It's a made-up gesture for bad actors.

I looked down at my fisted hands and grinned.

# CHAPTER THIRTY-ONE

G abrielle Hays lived on Elm Street south of Wilshire in Beverly Hills, often referred to by ironic residents as the Slums of Beverly Hills. It's very important to be north of Wilshire. That means you earn lots of money, you're successful, maybe even famous. I didn't peg Gabrielle for a mansion. But I did assume, with the career she's had, she'd have a home in the Hollywood Hills. Not the Spanish-style apartment house I slowly drove by in search of a parking place. I found one three blocks away.

Of course I had no proof she was involved in anything. But that hadn't stopped me from wheedling her address from a powerful woman I knew who threw parties and hosted political and charitable gatherings. I promised to donate to her newest cause: Save the Rattlesnakes. I wasn't sure if she meant the reptile kind or the human kind.

The building was a duplex with red bougainvillea vines crawling up its walls. She lived on the top floor. I followed the outdoor stairs up to her apartment and rang the bell. Nothing. I knocked. Nothing. I went back to my car.

Unless Gabrielle was shooting at night, she should come home soon. If it were me, I would. Exhausted, I'd be taking a bath, learning new lines, scraping some food together to eat. But I didn't get the role. She did.

I waited for the pinch of jealousy but felt nothing. Musing on this new reaction, I texted Heath:

> Gabrielle Hays, the actress, may be the other blonde. Going to talk to her.

Thinking of how we parted in front of Peter Bianchi's house, I wrote:

> Still angry with me?

Soon I got his response:

> I'm angry at having you back in my life. Be careful.

I loved the paradox of emotions in those two short sentences of his.

I tapped my fingers on the steering wheel. I'm not good at waiting. No patience. I decided I needed moisturizer. I could be dead broke but I'd still manage to buy the outrageously expensive stuff I put on my face. Call it vanity. Call it a waste. I call it maintenance.

I walked up Elm to Wilshire then down to Saks. Forty-five minutes later I had a tiny, tiny jar in a large silver box wrapped in tissue paper resting at the bottom of a shopping bag. And I'd signed an autograph. Alas, I'd also signed the receipt.

Now in the gray-lavender dusk I stood in front of Gabrielle's duplex. The lights were on. I decided to see how much she really wanted to meet with me. I took my cell out of my purse and called her.

When she answered, I said, "Hi, Gabrielle. It's Diana."

"Who?"

Give me a break. "Diana Poole. I'm in the neighborhood and thought I might stop by."

"Oh God, I'm in my trailer on the set." I could see her shadow move behind the window shade. "We're still shooting. They're calling for me now. Can't talk." She disconnected.

Maybe she just didn't like me and that's why she didn't want to see me. But, as I marveled at how much her silhouette resembled mine, I was beginning to believe she had a darker reason to avoid me.

At the top of her stairs, I rang the bell. She opened the door. I have to give her credit. It only took her a few seconds to get her shocked expression under control.

"What the hell's going on?" she demanded in her low, husky voice, holding a glass of wine.

"I told you I was in the neighborhood." I waved my Saks bag at her.

"I thought by my polite excuse you'd figure out I didn't want to see you. Were you standing right outside?"

"That wasn't an excuse. It was a big fat lie. And yes, I was standing outside."

She appeared to weigh possibilities, released a ragged sigh, and let me in. "Do you want some wine?" She took a long swallow of hers.

"I would love some."

She closed the door. Her glass tipping dangerously, she gestured toward a dining room chair out of place next to the small arched hearth. "Sit down." She disappeared behind an alcove.

Sitting, I looked around her small and sparsely decorated living room. Actors are nomads. Yet this room didn't represent a woman who wasn't home most of the time. It looked as if it belonged to a woman who'd been stripped of her belongings. There were dusty rectangles of lighter paint on one wall where paintings or photographs had once hung. I thought of the artwork at Moss & Becket. A less than half-empty bottle of white wine stood on the floor next to an expensive Eames lounge chair, which faced a small flat-screen balancing on a battered nightstand. Cables snaked down from their receptors into the wall socket. I heard a cupboard door slam beyond the alcove. Staring at the heap of ashes in the fireplace, I thought of my mother's ashes thrown around my husband's office. For the first time I realized what a rage-filled gesture that had been.

She walked back into the room with a jelly glass, took the bottle from the floor, filled the glass, then topped hers off.

"Here."

"Thanks." I took the wine.

Tucking her legs up, she curled into the curve of the leather Eames. A floor light shined on her blond hair and highlighted the heavy makeup she still wore from filming. Lines creased her kohl-rimmed eyes. The makeup man had shaded her cheekbones to accent their sharpness. Her lipstick was long gone, only a thin pencil line around the edges defined the downturn of her mouth. The shape of her lips made her look mournful and callous at the same time.

"So what did you buy at Saks?" She eyed the bag I'd placed on the floor next to me. Instead of looking comfortably elegant on her lounge, she looked very alone. A woman clinging to a raft in a dangerous sea.

"Moisturizer."

She took a long swallow of wine. "Don't you get tired of trying to hold back time?" She ran her free hand through her hair. It shimmered. Her face looked worn down.

"I'm not holding it back. I'm just not going to help it. I never had a chance to congratulate you on getting the role."

"Why would you? We never talk." She took the last swallow in her glass, reached down for the bottle, and poured herself the rest. "What do you want, Diana?" She was tipsy and trying not to slur her words.

"Are you happy being an actress?" That wasn't what I'd intended to say at all. The words just came out as if they'd always been there waiting to be asked. But who was I really asking?

"I was when I first came out here. I clicked right away. No waitressing for me. I got a small part in a major movie. The director said he liked me because I wasn't a true beauty. My face was complicated. He told me that in bed. I never worked with him again. But I kept getting bigger roles."

God, how depressingly clichéd every actor's story sounded, I thought. I sipped my wine.

She continued, "Then one day when I was shooting a TV commercial I realized I wasn't ever going to be an A-list actor. Let's face it, Diana, they wanted Cate Blanchett for the role we were up for. But they could never afford her. We'll always be on the second list. The At-Least-They-Save-The-Production-Money list." Laughing, she let her head fall back against the lounge. "Are *you* happy acting?"

"No," I heard myself say. "My agent's been calling me. I haven't called him back." Christ, had I come here to confess to Gabrielle Hays that I didn't want to act anymore?

"Did your mother leave you a pile of money?" I could hear the grin in her low voice. Or was it bitterness?

"No. Did *your* mother?"

Her head lifted sharply. Eyebrows arched. I held her gaze. She raised her glass to take another drink then realized it was empty. Reaching for the bottle, she saw it was empty too. "I'll get us more wine. And pretzels. I must remember to eat."

She stumbled as she got up, found her balance, grabbed the empty bottle, and swayed through the alcove again.

Wondering how she was able to work with a hangover, I stared at two closed doors next to the fireplace. From the kitchen I heard the refrigerator door open and then slam shut. She mumbled something. Or maybe she was singing. I set my glass on the floor and went to the doors.

Opening one, I peered into Gabrielle's bedroom. The top of a white wicker dresser was scattered with makeup, a hairspray can, brushes, and a dog-eared script. Slippers, run down at the heels, lay on the floor beside an unmade queen-size bed. I heard the pop of a cork from the kitchen. Closing the door, I opened the other one.

It felt cold, like Colin's office. A room of the dead. There was a single bed stripped of its linen. Human stains soiled the mattress. There was no other furniture. Boxes and trash bags lined one wall. I moved toward them. The boxes were taped shut. I opened one of the trash bags and pulled out an orange caftan. Elizabeth Rodgers had died wearing a blue one. I shoved it back in and pushed my hand deeper into the bag. I felt something starched and crumpled. I dragged it out and shook it. It was a baby's christening gown.

A high piercing animal sound froze me. Gabrielle, lips drawn back, eyes narrowed to slits, rushed at me holding the chardonnay bottle by the neck like a club. Wine poured down her arm and the front of her T-shirt onto her jeans. Dropping the infant's dress, I raised my arms to block the blow.

# CHAPTER THIRTY-TWO

The bottle of wine slid out of Gabrielle's raised hand. It fell with a thud and rolled toward the corner. We stared wild-eyed at each other. I lowered my arms. They ached with tension, with the anticipation of a blow. The smell of wine permeated the room. She turned and lunged toward a door, threw it open, and rushed into the bathroom. Flicking on the light, she leaned over the sink and retched into the basin. I looked away.

Hearing water running, I peered back as Gabrielle rinsed her face and mouth, then grabbed a towel and wiped her lips and the dark crescents of mascara under her eyes.

"Can I get you anything?" I asked.

"You can leave."

"I didn't mean to upset you, but I have to know something. When we met in the stairwell, before you read for the part, you asked me about the accident on PCH. You knew it happened in front of my house."

"It was on the news." She pressed her hands down on the vanity's tile rim and stared at her reflection in the mirror. "It was just conversation."

"You and I never talked. Never had a conversation before. Naturally, I wondered why the death of that woman was so important to you."

"Did I say it was?"

"You looked sad. Tired. I've never seen you look that way."

She lowered her gaze to the sink, hands still gripping the edge.

"I found an orange caftan in the bag of clothes."

She lurched from the vanity to the doorjamb. "You found? You sneaked in here and searched through my things."

"Elizabeth Rodgers had a blue caftan on when she died."

"Why are you still here?"

"I need to know about her, Gabrielle."

"Do you think witnessing some woman's death gives you the right to know everything about her life? My life?"

"When it affects me. Yes."

Her mouth curved down, making her look sullen. Her eyes narrowed. "She was a drunk. She was my mother."

"I'm sorry."

"Because she was a sot and a slut? Or because you witnessed her death?"

"Because she died."

"Her death is a relief." She brushed past me and sat on the end of the bed and asked, "Did you feel relief when your mother died?"

"I thought I would. But no, I didn't."

"I spent a fortune putting her in rehab centers. But she'd run away, or if she stayed the thirty or ninety days until she was released, then the cycle would start all over again. Sometimes a bartender would call and tell me to come pick her up. Once a stranger did. He said he had to go to work, but he'd leave his door unlocked for me. I found her lying naked on the guy's bed, bruises on her thighs and arms. I dressed her and took her home." She studied me in her superior way and finally said, "Is that enough information for you?"

"I want to know why she was so afraid of someone that she chose to walk into traffic. I want to know why she had my mother's bracelet in her hand."

"Bracelet? What kind of bracelet?"

"It was gold-link with a diamond scorpion charm."

"Scorpion. Sounds ugly."

"My mother's birth sign. Very expensive."

"I never saw it. Your mother died at the Bel Air, right? Maybe they ran into each other in the bar there, and she gave it to her. Or maybe my mother stole it. Anything is possible with a drunk. I have to get out of this room."

We started toward the living room. I stopped and picked up the infant's christening gown. "Shall I just leave this on the bed?"

She turned back and started to gesture toward the bare ugly mattress as if I should leave it there, then seemed to change her mind. She took it from me. "My mother was afraid of a ghost. This belonged to my sister, Lizzie. She was six when she died. My mother kept it. Carried it around to remind her how careless drunks can be."

I waited for her to continue.

Gabrielle held the small gown against her body, smoothing it with one hand. "My mother was napping. That's what Lizzie and I called it. She was really passed out on the sofa. Lizzie and I were in the front yard. It was summer. She was running through the sprinklers playing with a beach ball. I was ten, sitting on the porch. I was supposed to watch Lizzie. But I was bored and thirsty. I went inside to get us some Cokes." Tears filled her eyes. "The screech of the car's tires was so sharp, so piercing that it even woke my mother from her stupor. Lizzie had run after the ball. Killed instantly. I wasn't surprised my mother finally ended her life by walking in front of a car."

She laid the dress out on the bed. I believed her story. I had no reason not to. But watching her gently fold the baby dress and tuck the yellowed arms into the long skirt, I remembered I had found it stuffed thoughtlessly into a plastic garbage bag. Like everything with Gabrielle, even her acting, there was the presence of a distorting shadow. Maybe that's what made her so good.

I'd had enough, though. I was drained and wanted to get out of her tortured life.

"Did you break into my house?" I asked flatly.

Her head jerked up. "What?"

"A witness saw a blond woman who looked like me from the back going into my house. Later I found someone had ransacked my house. I think the blonde was looking for the bracelet."

"You're accusing me of burglary?"

"Attempted."

"And why would I do that?"

"As I told you, the scorpion bracelet is valuable. StarView is very expensive. And you must have other bills."

"You're a sick, jealous woman, Diana." She stalked into the living room. I heard the front door opening. I went in and took my purse from where I'd left it.

Standing by her opened door, she said, "It's June gloom, Diana. There's fog everywhere. I feel like it's inside of me."

I stepped out into the damp thick mist. The door slammed shut behind me.

As I walked back to my car, confused, emotions on edge, I realized I'd forgotten my moisturizer.

# CHAPTER THIRTY-THREE

Kiki's was quiet tonight. Most of the tables and booths were empty. The candles in the hurricane lamps flickered and reflected off the surfboards hanging on the walls like pieces of sculpture. I was tucked in a small booth. This was how I liked it here. Calm. Cozy.

From his perch at the end of the bar, Kiki raised his ubiquitous cup of coffee to me. I raised my red wine to him. He was a small wiry man, skin tanned to a buckskin color and covered in tattoos. Notes to himself, he called them. His bleached-blond nappy hair made him appear as if he was wearing a yellow knit cap.

Staring into my wine, I sifted through my disturbing encounter with Gabrielle Hays. I thought of her rushing at me with the raised bottle in her hand. Would she have struck me? I thought so at the moment. I felt her rage bearing down on me. Her frenzy. But she didn't strike. Why not? And then there was her emotional, painful story about her mother and her sister, which I did believe.

Kiki appeared at my table with a bottle. "You look hungry. I've ordered you a hamburger rare."

Smiling at him, I realized I was starving. "Thank you. You know if I had a father, he'd be like you."

Kiki threw his head back and let out his high whinny laugh. He topped off my glass and retreated to his place at the bar.

I took another sip. When Gabrielle had rushed at me I was holding her dead sister's christening gown. I'd reminded her of a horrible memory. But why would that memory make her violent? And why was the tiny gown stuffed in the garbage bag if it was so dear to her? And what did any of this have to do with her breaking into my house? She was vehement in her denial. And I was beginning to question myself about that. Maybe Gabrielle just didn't like me digging around in her painful life. Maybe she just didn't like me. At this moment I couldn't blame her.

I leaned my head back. My eyes came to rest on a large man with a shock of wild gray hair, wearing a tweed jacket, hunched over his drink at the bar. Grabbing my wine, I got up, walked to the bar, and slid onto the stool next to him.

"Do you come here often?" I smiled and winked.

Dr. Sam Walford turned in my direction and blinked his thoughts away. "Ms. Poole."

"Diana."

"Diana." His deep Shakespearean voice repeated my name. "No. I don't come here often." He chuckled. "I was working late. Tired, I guess. Before the long drive home, I came in for a drink and ordered coffee instead. It's damn good, by the way." He patted my hand. It was large and warm.

"That's because it's Kiki's special blend."

"He should go into business like Starbucks."

"He thinks they're the Madonna of coffee."

His brow wrinkled. "I'm not sure what that means."

"Not the real thing. Where is home for you?"

"Not in Malibu."

"You were deep in thought. Would you like me to leave you alone?"

"God, no. Save me from my contemplations." He peered down his hawk-like nose at me. "You look much more pulled together than the last time I saw you at StarView."

"Maybe because I'm not covered in dirt and wearing sweats."

"You really are quite beautiful," he said matter-of-factly.

'Thank you."

"You remind . . ." He stopped, then said, "You handle your beauty well."

"You were going to say I remind you of my mother. But you thought better of it. Afraid of my shaky ego?"

"I think your ego is quite healthy."

"I'm glad to hear it."

He sipped his coffee.

"I have a problem," I said into my wine.

"You're looking for free advice?"

"No. Well, maybe."

He turned toward me, giving me his full attention. "What's your problem?"

I met his eyes. "Gabrielle Hays."

Surprised, he asked, "Elizabeth Rodgers's daughter?"

I nodded. "Have you met her?"

"Of course. We talked about her mother's death."

"I saw her this evening."

"Are you friends?"

"Oh, no. What did you think of her?"

"What's all this about, Diana?"

"I feel I might have been wrong about her. But I'm not sure."

He grinned. "And you want to talk about your inability to admit a mistake?"

I laughed. "No. I want to talk about her. She's not a patient of yours, is she?"

"No."

"But you know her history. I mean through her mother."

"What did she tell you?"

I told him about her mother's ugly bout with alcoholism and the death of her daughter, Gabrielle's sister.

"I'm surprised she opened up to you that much. The few times I've talked with her I had the feeling that Gabrielle was living out of fear. Many children of alcoholics are brought up in great distress. Fear of the unexpected. Fear of abandonment. Fear that a parent having one more drink can change the fragile hold they have on life forever. Gabrielle has built a strong defense against all of that. It keeps her safe, but it also pushes people away so they can't hurt her."

"I may have forced her to open up. Unintentionally, of course. Well, that's not true. I was prying."

"Ah."

"Do you say that a lot to your patients?"

"Sometimes I say 'oh,' 'uh-huh,' or 'hum.' And if I'm feeling very verbal, I'll say, 'I see' or 'go on.'"

"I have the feeling you say more than that to the people you're helping. Do you know where Gabrielle was the night of her mother's death?"

"Matter of fact I do. She was on her way to StarView to take Elizabeth out to dinner. I'd recommended it."

"That's why Elizabeth Rodgers was wearing Spanx."

"I beg your pardon?" He peered at me questioningly.

"Underwear that slims you."

"Really?"

"Don't men know anything about what women wear under their clothes?"

His eyes turned impish. "Let's just say the practicalities of women's undergarments to a man are how quickly said man can take them off."

I grinned. "True. Nonetheless it was something that bothered me. Why would a woman wear it under a caftan? But if she were going out, it makes sense."

"A problem solved." He sounded delighted. A man who lived to unravel problems.

"Was Gabrielle at StarView when her mother ran away?"

"No. In one those cruel twists of fate she was stuck in traffic on PCH due to her mother's death. But she didn't know what the cause was at the time. The police made her turn around, and she had to go back home. She called StarView to tell them she couldn't get there. Reception put her call through to me." He sighed. "I told her what had happened. Or what I knew at the time."

"How did she take it?"

"Like a daughter who couldn't believe her mother was dead."

"Do you always see the good in people, Doctor?"

"I mostly see the darkness. The pain. The regret. Horrible things that can't be undone. But I'm like an old Hollywood movie. At the end there's always something good to come out of the human wreckage."

"Human wreckage. Is that what we all are?"

"Some of us."

I looked at him sharply. His bright, intelligent eyes were shadowed. With what? Memory? Sadness?

"Do you feel part of that wreckage?" I asked.

"Did I imply that?"

"You said 'us.'"

"Ambivalence."

"What do you mean?"

"You can feel part of that human wreckage and still feel blessed. Or bliss, if you prefer."

I said, "I got the feeling Gabrielle's desperate for money."

"Isn't she shooting a very big movie now?"

"Yes. But she had to pay for all these clinics her mother was in. She must owe StarView."

"I try not to get involved in the financial affairs of StarView. But I know Marc Decker and Ms. Hays are working out an arrangement on how much she's due after her mother's death."

"You mean she was going to sue him?"

"Elizabeth is the first patient we've had who wandered or ran away and died. Gabrielle will come out a fairly wealthy woman."

"Well, that takes away the motivation for her to break into my house."

"What?" He set down his cup with such force that coffee slopped over onto the bar.

"A blond woman who looks like me from the back broke into my house. I think she was looking for the scorpion bracelet."

Grabbing a cocktail napkin, he mopped up the mess he'd made. "Why would Gabrielle Hays want it?"

"I thought because her mother had it. Because she needed money. But after what you just told me, I'm beginning to think I made a mistake."

"How did you know it was a blond woman? Were you there?"

"No. There was a witness who saw a blond woman go into my house. A man was with her. This witness thought the woman was me. Nothing was taken. I have the bracelet in a safe place. There was an engraving on the tail of the scorpion. It said 'To B. Your B.'"

"Your mother's name doesn't begin with a B."

"No. I'm thinking about love. Beauty and the Beast."

"The fairy tale?" His head tilted, bushy dark eyebrows lifted.

"Yes. The fairy tale. In your view of human wreckage, does the beast remain a beast?"

He thought a moment, then said, "No. The beast turns into a prince. But the prince is left with a lot of beast baggage."

We both laughed. Then it faded and turned into a not uncomfortable silence.

He looked at his watch then at me. As if debating with himself, he shifted his kind, penetrating eyes to mine. "Would you do me a favor?"

"If I can."

"Will you stop sleuthing?"

"What? Why?"

He put an avuncular hand on my cheek. "I worry about you." He withdrew it quickly and slid off the stool. Then he fumbled in his pants pocket for cash and tossed it on the bar.

"Why are you worried about me?" I persisted.

Adjusting his jacket, he said, "When you sat down next to me I was thinking about the death of poor Gerard Quincy."

"They say it's suicide. Do you believe that?"

"I believe the man is dead. And he didn't deserve to die."

"Are you saying I'm in danger?"

"I can worry about people who aren't in danger. It's a work hazard. I especially worry about the ones I like."

I watched him leave. Large and shambling. Jacket crumpled. Unruly shaggy hair. He pulled open the door and the cool foggy air wafted in. Then the door closed and he was gone.

I stared at his empty coffee cup and took another sip of my wine. He didn't ask for more explanation about the engraving on my mother's bracelet. I glanced at the door again. He wanted me to stop sleuthing. He was worried about me. But yet I wasn't in danger. It didn't make sense. And he was a man who made sense. I got up and went after him.

Slipping out the entrance, I saw Walford, his back to me, waiting on the corner of Windswept Road and PCH. A limo, a long black shadow in the heavy mist, sailed down the side street. Quickly stepping out of the light, I watched it edge to the curb. The driver, muscled and bald-headed, got out. As Walford reached to open the back door, the driver roughly grabbed his hand, stopping him. The driver opened it. No interior light went on. Shoulders slumping, Walford got in. Was there somebody else in the backseat? Was Tanya in the front? Just shadows. The driver slammed the door closed, then wedged himself back behind the wheel. The limo pulled away from the curb and turned left on PCH heading south.

I ran for my car to follow them, then stopped. I didn't have my purse. My keys. A hand gripped my shoulder. I whirled around, ready to defend myself. It was Kiki. "Your hamburger is getting cold. You need to eat."

# CHAPTER THIRTY-FOUR

I sat on the end of my bed, calling Ryan on my cell. The small amount of hamburger I ate under Kiki's stern gaze felt like a fist in my stomach.

When Ryan answered, I asked, "Is Tanya there?"

"Don't tell me you want to speak to her." I could hear the surprise in his voice.

"No. I just want to know if she's there."

"Don't start, Diana."

"Just tell me."

"No. She's with clients."

I thought if I explained what I had seen outside Kiki's it would only cause more problems between us. Instead I said, "Thanks. Hope I didn't wake you up."

"You got me in the middle of writing. You all right?"

"I'm fine. I'm glad you're writing."

"It feels good. Good night."

"Good night." I disconnected.

I looked at my phone screen. It was 10:08. He sounded sober and was writing. And I was chasing a limo filled with shadows.

Restless, I got up and wandered through the house. I had to do something. I opened the door to Colin's office, the one room I hadn't picked up since my house was ransacked. Avoidance. Who wants to vacuum up their mother's ashes? A rhetorical question.

I moved to a closet door by the bathroom, opened it, and took out a vacuum cleaner. I plugged it in, and it roared to life. Over the howling noise, I said to my mother's gray tossed remains, "You always had a great sense of irony. So I hope you can see the humor in this." I felt my heart clench as I shoved the vacuum across the floor, sucking up her ashes, and pushing through the clothes and papers I should have picked up first.

I thought of Walford getting into the limo. Why didn't he just tell me a car was picking him up? I pushed the vacuum around a box; it gobbled up something that made it rattle, then it continued smoothly along. Walford wanted me to stop sleuthing. He said he was worried about me. Why? I turned off the vacuum. It shuddered to silence. I leaned on it, staring at the three Oscars on Colin's desk. I was going to have to dust them. Feeling sorry for myself, I thought it was unfair that the living had to clean up after their dead. Then I felt a pricking on the back of my neck. A creased photo was propped up against one of the Oscars. My mother's.

I picked it up. My skin grew tight across my forehead and temples. It was the picture I had found in the pocket of my mother's robe when I was going through her things. She was still holding my hand. We were still smiling.

How did it end up on the desk? I'd been drunk and crying, thinking I'd finally found a clue. A clue that my mother still thought of me. Loved me. A poignant clue a drunken daughter finds and sobs over. But when sober she would smile sadly at it and take it in her stride. Except now. I knew I had not placed this picture on the desk.

I needed to talk with somebody who was objective. With an unsteady hand, I placed the photo back exactly the way I found it.

I called Heath.

In the kitchen, I made coffee. My body throbbed as if I'd run into a wall. I sat down at the table and waited for the coffee to brew and Heath to arrive. I was trying to keep my wild thoughts in check.

I thought of my mother. There is always another blonde.

# CHAPTER THIRTY-FIVE

eath studied the photo of my mother and me that was propped up against her Oscar. Wearing a wrinkled gray T-shirt under a black bomber jacket, hair slightly mussed, he looked as if he'd dressed quickly. He rubbed the back of his neck and asked, "Can you show me the robe you found this in?"

"That one." I gestured to the silk wrap crumpled on the floor. He picked it up. The stains of vomit and illness were still visible. "Except I found it in a taped box with some of her other clothes. I pulled the robe out and found the picture of us in the pocket."

"What did you do with it then?"

I'd been drinking. I couldn't remember. "I cried."

"Okay." He waited.

"Actually it was a crying jag. I was drunk. I couldn't go through her past and mine sober."

"So you don't remember what you did with the photo?"

"I'm almost sure I put it back in the pocket. And stuffed the robe back in the box."

"Almost?"

"I know I didn't prop it up against her Oscar."

"Why?"

"It's not something I'd do."

"But you said you were drunk."

"Remind me again why I called you?"

A slight grin. "So you think whoever broke into your house took the photo and tossed it on the desk."

"Not tossed. It was purposely placed there so it'd be seen. By me."

He folded the robe neatly and laid it on top of a box, then he moved around the room dragging his fingers over the gray film.

"I'm not crazy."

He squatted down by some ashes I hadn't yet cleaned up. He sifted through them, rubbing his fingertips together. He rose up, grabbed the empty urn and swept his hand around inside of it. Then he took the vacuum cleaner and emptied the contents of its bag onto the floor. Dust rose up, small pieces of ash settled. He crouched and ran his fingers through the debris.

He stood. "Give me some of that coffee you're drinking."

In the kitchen I filled a mug for him while he washed his hands at the sink. We sat at the table facing each other.

Heath took a long, thoughtful swallow. Dark stubble with flecks of gray covered the lower half of his face. "There's no bone in the ash."

"What?"

"When a body is cremated the bones don't completely disintegrate. There's usually fragments mixed in with the ashes. Sometimes fingernails. Even hair. But bones, mostly."

I sat back. "Oh, my God. Then you're saying my mother is alive."

"Isn't that what you were thinking?"

"Yes. But . . . yes." I let out my breath. "It's still a shock. What kind of ash was in the urn?"

"Probably from a fireplace. When you called me to come over here you told me you ruled out Gabrielle Hays."

"She had no reason to break in. Elizabeth Rodgers is her mother. She's working out a settlement with StarView over her death."

"Elizabeth Rodgers is Gabrielle's mother?" He raised his brows. "Good work."

"Thank you," I said bleakly. Standing, I went to the sink, turned on the faucet, and threw cold water on my face. I grabbed a dishtowel and buried my face in it.

"Are you all right?" Heath asked.

I raised my head. "My mother was a pain in the ass to live with," I snapped, blinking away tears. "I don't know if I want her back."

"It looks like she wants you to find her."

"Well, let's do it," I sobbed.

Sitting back down at the table, I wiped away my tears with the dishtowel. He took his notepad from the pocket of his bomber jacket.

"Do you remember the name of the crematorium?"

"No. I never went there. I was out of town. They sent the urn to the Bel Air Hotel. I picked it up there."

"There are a lot of sleazy crematoriums. They're probably long gone."

"I've seen her, Heath. I didn't know it at the time."

"Go on."

"In Starbucks waiting for Gerard Quincy. I was sitting by the plate glass window. A limo drove in and parked by the entrance. Its headlights shined in right on me. I was spotlighted like a diva. Then Tanya comes in and the limo backs away from the window down toward the end of the parking lot. When Tanya got back into the limo, the interior light went on. I glimpsed a couple in the back. They weren't clear. But I did see blond hair. I remember thinking they were either embracing or struggling."

"You think your mother was in the car, saw you, and that's why they backed away?"

"Yes."

"If you're right, then that means Tanya is in on this."

"But we have no proof. She'll just say it was her clients in the backseat. Don't tell Ryan yet."

"I'm working for him."

"He won't believe us. And I don't want him to get hurt."

Heath rubbed the side of his cheek. I could hear the scraping sound of his fingers against the stubble. "How much time was there between the limo leaving Starbucks and you returning home?" he asked.

"If there's light traffic, my house is about eight minutes away. I waited about an hour after they left. They had time to break in."

"Why would your mother do that?"

"She had to be forced. She had to be afraid. That's why she propped up the photo on the desk."

"And they were looking for the scorpion bracelet."

"Yes. If they found the bracelet then there would be no connection to my mother. Another reason for her to leave the picture."

"Can you describe the man who was with your mother in the back of the limo? Anything at all?"

"She was blocking him. But I can tell you who I think he was."

"Who?"

"Dr. Sam Walford. Again I don't have any proof."

"Then tell me your feelings."

Surprised, I said, "You rarely ask about feelings."

"Maybe I'm learning from an actress I know." His dark, somber eyes took me in.

I rested my forehead in my hands, gathering my thoughts. "I ran into him at Kiki's tonight," I said, looking up. "Here's how I felt. I absolutely adored him. If I could curl up in his lap I would.

He's intelligent. Witty. Self-deprecating. And giving. Everything a woman wants in a man."

"But you think he kidnapped your mother."

"I think he was in the limo with her."

"Did you ask him about the engraving on the scorpion?"

"Yes. And like everybody else he said Nora's name doesn't begin with the letter B, as if I didn't know that."

He flipped though his notes. "Dr. Patel said the exact same thing. They're consistent."

"Or they got their stories straight. I think Walford's the beast. I have nothing to back this up with except. . ."

"Except?"

"He's big. Shaggy. Lumbering but balanced, even graceful. Like a beast in the forest might be. That's why I followed him outside the bar. He got into the same limo. I recognized the bald-headed driver."

"Anybody else in the car?"

"Shadows. It's been almost a year since she died. Or didn't die."

"People have been held longer."

"Walford wanted me to stop sleuthing."

"Did he give a reason?"

"He was worried about me."

"Or worried you might find your mother." He stood, slipping his pen and notebook back into his pocket. "You're tired. You need sleep."

.I walked him to the door. We stood, both of us exhausted but with questioning looks in our eyes.

Finally I said, "I don't want my mother dead. But for Christ's sake, she slept with my husband."

Heath reached out, slid his hand behind my head, and pulled me to him. He leaned down and kissed me. Then he stepped back.

"What was that for?"

"It was either to comfort you or to shut you up about your mother. Meet me at Patel's clinic at nine in the morning. After all, he signed your mother's death certificate." He opened the door and left.

# CHAPTER THIRTY-SIX

I didn't have a good feeling. Patel's clinic was closed. It was 8:30 in the morning and I sat in my car staring at the joyful blue building, thinking that working mothers and fathers would depend on the clinic being open early, but no one was outside waiting.

Fifteen minutes later Heath pulled his car up behind mine. He got out, opened my door, and slid in next to me.

"Your doors are unlocked," he said.

"The locks aren't working today. Maybe they will tomorrow."

"Christ, Diana."

"Good morning."

He smiled. "Good morning. Looks like the clinic is closed."

"It is. I haven't seen anyone."

He smelled of fresh soap and was shaved. "You'd think they'd be open at this hour. We'll wait."

"I couldn't sleep last night. I kept wanting to reach for the phone and call the police."

"You're not going to like this, but I'm going to talk to you like a Hollywood fixer. If you call the police it will leak to the press. The press will have an orgasm. Think of it. The daughter of Nora Poole believes her dead mother, after all this time, has really been kidnapped. Is Diana Poole having a nervous breakdown after her young lover Peter Bianchi rejected her?"

I remembered Marc Decker had said something similar to me. "Nice one, Heath."

"You know I'm right. Besides, I beat the crap out of Bianchi. That's not going to look good either. We'll find her, Diana."

"I know."

He shifted his body and settled back in his seat. "Why did you stop the affair with Bianchi?"

"You already asked me that."

"No. I asked how you could have an affair with him. Now I'm asking why you stopped it."

"Because I didn't like myself very well. You ever have that problem with a woman, Heath? Where you began to hate yourself for staying with her?" Waiting for his answer, I watched his jagged profile.

"Maybe. Here comes Patel's nurse."

I followed his gaze to Miss Bell walking down the sidewalk to the clinic. She wasn't wearing her teddy bear–print scrubs this morning. Instead she was dressed in a long pink skirt and red tank top with a bright purple scarf wrapped around her head. But the brilliant colors couldn't hide her sadness. She walked stiffly, as if her body was too heavy for her to endure. She stopped at the clinic's entrance, taking keys from her large purse.

"Let's go," Heath said.

We hurried out of the car just as she opened the door. Stepping inside, she whirled around, pink skirt flaring, and recognized us. She started to slam the door in our faces. But Heath shoved his shoulder between her and the jamb.

She staggered backward, eyes wide and angry as hell. "I knew you were no damn good." She aimed her words at me as I moved inside, closing the door. "And get off my mail." She glared down at my feet.

Scattered around my shoes were envelopes with officious-looking return addresses from Medicaid and insurance companies. I picked them up, and handed them to her.

She grabbed them and slapped them down on the reception counter.

"We need to speak to Patel," I said.

"Does it look like he's here?" She gestured to the ghostly room.

"Then we need to know where he is." Heath removed his sunglasses and put them in his jacket pocket.

"Would you like to know where the children are? Where they're being taken care of?" She shook her head angrily. "In emergency rooms, waiting with crackheads and men bleeding from knife and gunshot wounds."

I glanced at the pile of old toys shoved into the corner. "I'm sorry. I never meant . . .," I faltered. Christ, what could I say?

"I don't want your apologies." She laid a large hand on the counter and looked Heath up and down. "Patel's in India. You people have all the answers. Go find him."

"That's a long way away," Heath said.

"It's his homeland."

I eyed the closed door next to the reception counter. Opening it, I started down the hallway.

"You think he's hiding under his desk?" she yelled after me.

Everything in Patel's office that was personal was gone, even the children's drawings. The big heavy wooden drawers in his school-principal's desk hung opened and empty.

"We're too late," I said to Heath, who stood in the doorway. "Maybe he *is* in India."

"Maybe."

He turned and walked down the hallway, opening doors and peering into examining rooms. Miss Bell had gone behind the counter and was now sitting at her desk going through the mail as if we weren't there.

"Where does he live?" Heath asked her.

"You forgot this one." She waved a letter at the door behind her.

It opened onto narrow steep stairs. I followed Heath up into a pitched-roof attic. A piece of gold silk was draped across the only window. The sun burrowed through it, transforming the color of the room and the rough wood floor into hot saffron. Under the window was a mattress. Next to it was a half-burnt candle cradled in a lotus-leaf holder. Heath pulled back a blue-and-white madras curtain to reveal a bare clothes rod attached to the wall.

"He said he wanted to live humbly." Miss Bell filled the doorway. "Then mentioned something about Gandhi."

"What's Patel's cell phone number?" Heath asked.

"When he moved to this end of town, he threw his phone into the L.A River. It's not very deep. Probably bone dry with the drought now. You might still find it there."

"There had to be times you needed to talk to him," Heath persevered. "Emergencies with his patients."

She nodded at a landline phone sitting on the floor next to the bed. "The clinic's phone number is on there."

"Did he have voice mail or an answering machine?"

"I took his messages."

"What about visitors?" I asked.

She shrugged. "What did he do that was so terrible that he left that posh place to open a clinic here?"

"He may have forged my mother's death certificate."

Her brow furrowed. "I don't understand."

"He was treating my mother. She was kidnapped. But Dr. Patel pronounced her dead and signed her death certificate."

She shook her head "No. Not him."

"I'm afraid so."

"Then he had his reasons. Good reasons. If you two are through banging around here, leave. I have work to do."

"Maybe he did do it for a good reason," I said, trying to find a way to get more information from her. "If I could find my mother, she'd tell me. Maybe we could work things out so he could come back."

"Do I look like a fool?" Her eyes blazed.

"No." I spoke quickly. "I think you love those children he was caring for. If you know something that might help me, there's a chance it might help Dr. Patel too."

"I don't know anything."

"If *your* mother was kidnapped, what would you do?"

"I'd thank the Lord. She was a drunk and an addict."

Christ. Were there no sober mothers? "So was mine. Well, a drunk. Not an addict."

Her eyes narrowed. "Dr. Patel was trying to help her?"

"I think they were trying to help each other."

"Then why would he forge her death certificate?"

"I don't know. That's one of the reasons I want to find her."

"Maybe someone visited him here," Heath said. "Someone he talked to. A friend."

"No." She looked away from him and I knew she was lying.

"Please tell me," I said.

"I don't want any trouble for him."

"Can you describe him?"

"Tall. Gray hair. Kind. Look like he needed to be dry-cleaned." Her hand went to her purple scarf. "He told me I should wear bold colors because I was a brave woman. He gave me this." She stroked the brightly colored scarf she wore and beamed for a moment.

It sounded like something Walford would say. "Was his name Dr. Walford?"

"Yes. He was good with the children. They loved his visits."

"How often did he come here to see Patel?" Heath asked.

She shrugged. "They always went out for lunch. I don't know what Dr. Patel did at night. Did Dr. Walford run away too?"

"Why do you ask?" I said.

"Walford was a good man. So was Patel, and now Patel's gone. I thought maybe whatever happened had forced Walford to leave too. Crazy. It's usually the bad ones who run." She picked up the hem of her bold pink skirt and went back down the stairs.

"Let's go to StarView and have another talk with Walford." I turned to Heath. "It *is* crazy. They *are* good men."

# CHAPTER THIRTY-SEVEN

don't think either one of you made an appointment, did you?"
Eddie, with the pool boy eyes, waited in the shade of the rambling Cape Cod porch, a big smile planted on his face. Heath and
I had just reached the top of the cobblestone driveway and found
him waiting for us.

"So those cheap cameras you have on the gate below aren't just
for show." Heath grinned.

"Nothing's for show here," Eddie replied, bouncing down the
porch stairs toward us. The feather around his neck fluttered. On
the swath of lawn a yoga class was going through warrior poses.

"I hoped Dr. Walford might be able to see us," I said.

"He's not here."

Surprised, I asked, "Where is he?"

"It's his day for seeing private patients."

"Do you know where Walford's office is?" Heath asked.

"I'm not sure of the address. I can call him and get it. Let him know you're coming." He pulled a cell phone from the pocket of his jeans, scrolled, and punched a number.

After a few moments he spoke, "Hi, this is Eddie, Dr. Walford." I noticed his voice pitched higher. He gestured awkwardly with his free hand. It's always the arms and hands that give non-actors problems. "I just want to let you know that Diana Poole and Leo Heath want to come to your private office. I don't know what your schedule is . . ." He listened, smiled at me, then said, "Okay. I'll tell them. Hey, what's your address? Thanks." He disconnected and slipped the phone back into his pants pocket. "Dr. Walford said he'd be glad to see you on his lunch break at twelve thirty."

"And the address?" Heath prompted.

"Oh, sorry. It's a little bungalow he rents for an office." He gave us a number on Arizona Street in Santa Monica.

Heath and I started back down the drive. Eddie stayed with us. I didn't feel right about the call he made. Some people just can't act. Can't get outside of themselves.

"Beautiful day, isn't it?" Eddie was cheerful. "Fog broke early. Maybe we're finally through with June gloom."

"Do you know Dr. Patel?" I asked. "He's a colleague of Dr. Walford."

"Patel? That's an Indian name, isn't t?"

I nodded.

"No, can't say I do."

"What's the feather around your neck mean?" Heath wondered.

"Hope."

"For you?"

He laughed. "No, for our clients."

Heath studied him for a long moment as we reached the gate.

Eddie stayed on his side of StarView as if it was Shangri-La, and he was afraid to enter the real world for fear he'd turn into an old man and crumble to pieces.

"Something's not right about that phone call Eddie made," I told Heath as we walked off down the road.

"I know. Let's take my car."

We looked back at Eddie. He waved. I waved. He still had that smile planted on his face. In another five years, I thought that smile would turn stale, even surreptitious, because he used it too easily.

We got into Heath's car and belted up. He turned on the ignition and made a quick U-turn, speeding down Windswept. He just made the yellow light, and we careened onto PCH, headed toward Santa Monica.

I gripped the handlebar above the passenger window.

"You're right. Eddie wasn't talking to Walford," Heath said. "There was too much needless information. 'Meet you at your private office.' Why say that to Walford, who's supposedly already in his private office?" Heath weaved in and out of traffic.

"So he was warning someone that we're on our way to Walford's? But why?"

"You've rattled a lot of cages, Diana. Patel has left the country. Eddie's just doing his job. I assume it's for Marc Decker."

"But Decker doesn't have anything to do with Walford and my mother."

"Whatever it is, Walford's the golden goose that keeps clients coming to StarView. Maybe it's him he's worried about."

I remembered standing outside Kiki's and watching the limo driver roughly stop Walford from opening the door. Then doing it himself.

"The chauffer's some kind of security."

"They usually are."

We shot past the old white stucco building that was once a restaurant in the 1930s owned by the actress Thelma Todd. She was murdered in her garage. The police claimed it was suicide by carbon monoxide. She was blond too.

Heath veered off toward Santa Monica and wound his way along the busy streets. Through the window I watched people sitting at sidewalk tables drinking coffee, eating lunch, baseball caps shading their eyes, holding little dogs on their laps and chatting. Or staring at their cells.

"I want to see Walford alone," I said.

Heath made a left turn. "I don't think that's a good idea."

"I need to know if I'm right about him and my mother. He'll be more open with me."

"If he has—and that's a big *if*—kidnapped your mother, he may not want to talk with you now. He may be the one who wants Star-View protection."

"I saved your life. Remember?"

"I've never forgotten. *Fuck.* You're not going use that."

"I am."

I thought of Heath bound to a chair, blood running down his face and side, and I'm talking and talking to the bad guys. Acting my head off. Why do my best performances happen in real life?

Heath pulled to the curb a block from the address Eddie had given us. The bungalow was in a mixed-use area of medical high-rises, condos, apartments, and small homes.

"You have no scruples," he grumbled.

"You know I'm right to do this alone. Where will you be?"

"Where no one can see me."

"Like old times." I got out of the car.

# CHAPTER THIRTY-EIGHT

Walford's bungalow was an adobe brown color. Ferns splashed vivid green under the front window. Old camellia bushes, heavy with pink flowers, flourished on each side of the arched front door. As I approached, Walford opened it as if he'd been watching for me.

"I hope it wasn't too difficult to find a place to park," he greeted. "This used to be a quiet neighborhood. Now you can't find a parking place to save your life. It drives my patients crazy. No pun intended." He peered around. "Eddie said your friend Leo Heath would be joining us."

"I wanted to speak with you alone."

"Of course. Come in and sit down." Closing the door, he gestured to a comfortable-looking chair facing a library table piled with books and papers. "Can I get you some coffee? Or tea?"

"Coffee would be great."

As I sat down, Walford went into a small kitchen and eating area. He dominated the space with his size and expansive movements. Beyond the kitchen I could see a back door with a window. Through it was a wood fence with tumbling vines. A shadow darkened the view then disappeared quickly. Was it Heath?

Telling myself to relax, I looked around. His office was the living room. Bookcases covered every available wall space. Simple watercolors of flowers and ferns hung crookedly from nails hammered into the edges of the shelves. One was of the camellia bushes outside. A cracked-leather sofa ran along the front window. I was drawn to the room. Its warmth and lack of pretension made you want to spill your guts.

"I always try to keep a fresh pot going. My patients appreciate it." He returned with a big white mug in each hand. He set one down in front of me, took his, and sat across from me in his desk chair.

I'd always been comfortable with Walford, but not now. I felt only unease. He seemed to sense it, like a dog that knows when you're afraid of it.

"Sorry, I only have about forty-five minutes to give you." He gulped his coffee.

"That's all right." I drank mine. "A bungalow this size must have a bedroom and a bath." I smiled.

He chuckled. "One bed and one bath off the kitchen. The extent of my grand office." Was someone hiding in there? Waiting? I drank more coffee. He watched me with kind eyes.

"Did you do the watercolors?" I asked.

"I'm afraid so. I'm always reminded of Chagall's observation when he looked at an amateur's work and observed, 'Poor paint.'" He laughed, a low rumble. Turning serious, he leaned forward, put his arms on his desk, and clasped his hands. "It's always difficult to begin, isn't it? Even if you're not here for therapy."

He was a man who waited for another person's words to flood out so he could rearrange them into some kind of psyche-clarity for the adrift speaker. I wondered what he would do with my words.

"More difficult than I thought it'd be," I said. "Why did you ask me to stop sleuthing last night?"

"I was concerned for you."

"Not about what I might find out?"

His expression turned curious. "What is it you want, Diana?"

"Do you know a Dr. Patel?"

He thought a moment. "No, I can't say I do."

"He was my mother's doctor at the Bel Air Hotel. He signed her death certificate."

"Ah."

I forced a smiled. "You're making psychiatrist sounds."

He chuckled. "Force of habit."

"I talked to Dr. Patel. He told me how my mother had helped him to open a clinic for children."

"Your mother sounds like she was a good woman. More than just . . ." He hesitated.

"More than what?"

"A movie star."

"This morning I went back to talk to Dr. Patel and he had left the country for India, his homeland."

"Yes?" His eyes were still patient and kind.

"Miss Bell, his nurse, said he'd decided to leave after I came around asking about my mother. Why would he do that? I hadn't accused him of anything. Such as signing a death certificate for my mother, who might be alive."

His shoulders stiffened and his brow wrinkled with concern. "Diana, what exactly are you saying?"

"Miss Bell also said you'd been at the clinic. That you and Patel would go to lunch sometimes. By the way, Miss Bell was wearing the purple scarf you gave her. It's perfect for her. But then, you have a knack for selecting the right gift for the right person. Only my mother would see beauty in that scorpion. Beyond the diamonds, of course."

"Diana, I don't know what you're talking about. I don't know a Dr. Patel."

"Stop it. Don't lie to me!"

"Maybe I met him at a convention. There are many doctors . . ."

"There aren't many Miss Bells. When you first saw the scorpion in Marc Decker's office, you told me you thought it was a scarab. A man of your knowledge would know the difference between the two."

"You give me far too much credit."

"I'd have to trust you to give you credit for anything!" Furious, heart pounding, I jumped up, hurried through the kitchen, and threw open a door to a small bedroom and bath. I searched, even pulling back the shower curtain and yanking open a closet door. Then I opened the back door and peered around the yard. Okay, my mother wasn't hidden here. And there were no bad guys lurking in the shadows or the sun, or anywhere. I took a deep breath. Heath and I were wrong about Eddie and his call. I waited for our mistake to give me pause to rethink everything about Mother. But it didn't give me even a tick.

When I returned, Walford hadn't moved. He seemed frozen in time. "What are you looking for?" His voice was quiet.

"Some kind of thug Eddie called. Maybe to protect you or harm me. I don't know."

"I'd never harm you, Diana."

"I think you already have." I stood over him. "I know my mother is alive."

He clasped his large hands on the table and looked up at me. "If I tell you, will you stop searching?" I nodded, sitting back down.

He swiveled in his chair and studied the watercolor of the camellia bushes.

"I've always felt sorry for camellias. They're beautiful. Yet they have no aroma, no perfume radiates from them to dazzle us. Their heads seem to hang down in sorrow because they know this about themselves."

I waited. My heart beat faster, as if I were still searching empty rooms.

He turned back to me. "I felt the same thing when I first met Nora Poole. She'd lost something deep inside her. Her essence."

I let out my breath. "Where did you meet her?"

"She made an appointment to see me. I met her here. She sat where you're sitting."

"Why did she make the appointment?"

"That's all I can say. You know I'm not allowed to talk about a patient. The law is on my side here."

"How many bad people have hidden behind their vows and badges? Maybe there'd be fewer people killed in a movie theater or classroom if a shaking, cowardly psychiatrist had spoken up. Tell me, Doctor, has your precious Hippocratic Oath protected my mother?"

"No."

"Why did she pick you?"

He closed his eyes for long moment then opened them. "She'd heard I was the best. It took a few minutes for me to understand she didn't want help in a psychiatric way. She wanted to list her sins, as she called them."

"What were they?" My mouth felt dry. I took another sip of my coffee. It was cold now.

"I won't tell you, Diana. I won't break that trust." His face hardened. He shoved his coffee aside. "Let's just say she treated me more like a priest than a psychiatrist, except she wasn't looking for absolution. Maybe she just wanted to hear herself say those *sins* aloud to someone who could only tuck them away in his desk drawer and never reveal them. When she finished what she had come to say, she stood and asked, 'How much do I owe you?' I told her we weren't finished. She told me maybe I wasn't, but she was."

"What happened?"

"She told me to send the bill to where she was living. The Bel Air Hotel. I followed her outside and asked where she was going. She said, 'I'm going to drive around and look at the famous places that are no longer famous. Then I'm taking to my bed.' There was no doubt she was depressed."

"I want to hear something about her I don't know. You gave her the bracelet. Was that part of her therapy?"

"No."

"Well, then, you can talk about it."

"Diana . . ."

"Stop saying my name as if we've known each other for years. *The scorpion.* Tell me about it."

He sank back in his chair, somehow smaller. "I began to visit her at her suite. I got to know her. Nora said I looked like a beast. Her beast." He repeated the word fondly. "I found the bracelet in an antique shop and bought it on a whim."

"That's a lot of money for a whim. Maybe it was more of an obsession."

His eyes were steady on me. But his voice wasn't. "I loved her. I was a man who'd never been in love because he hadn't had the time or enough compassion left over from his work to give to another human being. And I was buying a ridiculously expensive, wonderfully odious scorpion for a woman who would adore it."

"How did Elizabeth Rodgers end up with it?"

"I don't know."

"Where is my mother? If you really are this good man you pretend to be, then tell me."

"Diana, you have to stop this. She's dead. Believe me, I tried to help her. We talked and talked. We fell in love, and I still couldn't save her."

"Then how do you explain fireplace ashes in her urn? How do explain that when she was forced to break into my house she left out a photograph for me to see."

He reached across the desk and grabbed my hands. "Look at me, death is safe."

"You're sick." I jerked my hands away from his grip and stood up with such force my chair fell backward, clattering on the floor. The front door flew open. Walford was on his feet. I whirled around and saw Heath standing there.

"You okay?" Heath asked me.

# CHAPTER THIRTY-NINE

Was I okay? No. Heath was driving up Windswept Road to my car. I had told him what Walford has said.

"I don't think he's crazy, Diana."

"You didn't see his eyes. He's taken her."

"There's too much that's doesn't make sense."

"Yes. Like our reaction to Eddie's phone call. There were no bad guys hiding in every corner of Walford's office and you didn't find any lurking in the neighborhood."

"It's not unusual when you're working a case to put meaning into an action that's not there." He pulled up behind my parked car and cut the ignition. "It was something Miss Bell said. You picked up on it."

"What?"

"She said something about Walford being a good man. And so was Patel, and he was gone now. She thought maybe Walford had to leave too."

"You're right. She thought it was usually the bad ones who ran. Not the good ones. What are you getting at?"

"Your instinct was to admire Walford. You never sensed he was crazy before. He told you, 'Death is safe.'"

"You think he's protecting my mother in some way?"

"Follow your instincts, Diana."

Maybe it was Heath's support of me. Or his insight. Or his damn strong profile. In any event, I leaned over to give him a kiss like he'd given me in the foyer last night. Except the kiss deepened and we were suddenly two teenagers in a car in Malibu in broad daylight struggling with passion and our clothes until we both managed to pull away, breathing as if it were our last breath.

We sat in silence. I was sure he was thinking of Madison, the Mystery Woman. I was thinking I'm not okay.

I got out of his car and got into mine and drove off.

Soon, I was sitting on my deck wearing my battered straw hat and staring out at the ocean. Death is safe. If it was so safe, why did my mother leave me a clue?

I gazed at my phone on the umbrella table. I picked it up and checked the messages I'd been avoiding. There were at least twenty from my agent. The first ones began with concern: *Are you all right? Call me. This is a big role. Lifetime wants you. Where are you? I'm worried about you!*

Then it went downhill: *You've screwed up, Diana. Big time. You made me and yourself look bad. Not professional. Where the hell are you? You better be dead.* The last one was simply: *F O.* I assumed that meant fuck off. Though he could have meant Fun's Over.

Why was I sabotaging my career while trying to find my mother? No, I wasn't okay.

I closed my eyes. If only sleep could make things better. If it were only true that all would be fine in the morning.

Then I heard their voices. Tanya's girly giggle and Ryan, the cynic in the sun, saying, "Are you trying to give me a heart attack?"

I sat up and took off my hat and watched them trudge through the sand to the water's edge. She wore a yellow tank top over low-riding gray sweat pants. He was in his usual outfit, except he was wearing tennis shoes, again very white ones. In tandem, they began to run, slowly at first, then faster.

He was almost keeping up with her now. She waved him on, and he was pumping for all his life. They disappeared around the curve of ocean out of my sight.

I leaped up and ran through my house into my bedroom. I scooped Ryan's key out of the bowl on my dresser. We shared house keys for when we were traveling. I was going to find out who the hell Tanya was.

Rushing back outdoors, I flew down my deck stairs and up his. I quickly unlocked his door. Stepping inside the quiet house, I locked it behind me and ran through his living room, stopping for a second to look around. Odd. It was immaculate. Ryan's man-boy clutter was gone.

I took the stairs two at a time and went directly to his bedroom. The bed was made. His bed was never made. His Uggs stood side by side at the end of it. His clothes weren't piled on the floor. The shelf that went around the entire room still displayed the toy train tracks and, when turned on, the Pullman that tooted along them. But it was free of dust. Christ, she was having a good effect on him.

On the decorator-chosen dresser, his cologne was lined up. A selfie of him and Tanya smiling in the late afternoon sun was framed in Mexican pressed tin. Her large orange leather bag sat next to it. I unzipped it and came out with a Tiffany designer gun. How image-conscious can one woman be? And why did she need a weapon? I set it on the dresser and continued to dig for a wallet. I found it. There were no credit cards, insurance cards, social security card, or driver's license. Nothing legal that would have her name on it. But there were neatly arranged bills from one to a thousand. I put her wallet next to the gun, then dug out her makeup kit and searched it. Nothing but lipsticks and such. Turning her purse over, I shook it. No receipts, no notes or business cards fell out. She had to have some kind of ID. I stopped. Listened. Heard just a house making its own peculiar noises.

Opening the top drawer of the dresser, I ran my hand under her neatly folded Victoria's Secret extra sexy bras and panties. The only thing I'd discovered was that Tanya was very well organized. As I returned her things to her bag, I noticed a small slit between the interior fabric and the leather exterior. It was just wide enough for me to slide two fingers down inside. I felt a laminated card. Pincer-like, my fingers eased it out. It was a driver's license. The photo was of Tanya, but the name on it was "Tina Andres."

Digging my phone out of my jeans pocket, I called Heath and gave him her name, address, and license number.

"I'll tell Rodriquez to get right on it. How did you find this out?"

I heard the downstairs door open and Ryan's and Tanya's voices.

"Later," I whispered, turning off my phone.

They were coming up the stairs, still talking. Shit. I started toward the bathroom to hide, then remembered they'd probably want to shower after a run. Breathless, I ducked into Ryan's closet just as they entered the room. I didn't have time to close the door all the way.

"You're getting so much faster, baby." Tanya sauntered into view, pulling her sweaty tank top off over her head. No sports bra for her. "Pretty soon you'll outrun me."

Ryan appeared behind her. "I don't want to outrun you. Come here." He turned her around and pulled her half-naked body to his and kissed her. Then he gently tried to push her head down his body.

Jesus, Ryan, not now.

"No, no, baby. I got an appointment with a client," Tanya cooed.

Relieved, I watched her pad out of my view.

Ryan stayed, turning to watch her. He looked upset. "Don't you want to give it up?"

"If I said I wanted to quit, I'd be lying." Her voice came from the bathroom. I heard the door close.

Letting out a sad sigh, Ryan's head drooped. My heart sank. Was he falling in love with her? I heard the shower turn on. Ryan lifted his chin, took a deep breath, and moved out of sight.

I frantically looked around the closet. Her clothes were hanging in here. I had to get out. Listening to the shower, I eased the door wider and stepped softly into the room. Ryan was sprawled on the bed, head propped up on pillows. We stared at each other for a brief moment.

He bolted up into a sitting position. Eyebrows shot up to his hairline. His mouth fell open.

I put my finger to my lips, shushing him, and as I crept past, his eyes bugged. His hair seemed to spring in all directions. Then shock turned to fury.

He swung his legs off the bed, and I bolted for the stairs.

"Diana!" He was right behind me, his voice low and furious. He grabbed the back of my blouse.

Pulling away, I whispered, "Not here. My house."

"Damn you, Diana!" he whispered behind me.

I was at the bottom of the stairs and I ran. I could hear his feet pounding behind me.

In seconds we were in my living room. Ryan's face was a dangerous red as he stormed around. I'd never seen him so angry.

"I . . . I . . . can't believe you broke into my house!" he sputtered.

"I didn't break in. I used your key."

He stopped his irate pacing and turned on me. He held out his hand. "Give it back."

"Ryan, please."

"Now!"

I dragged the key out of my pocket and dropped it on his palm.

"Her name isn't Tanya," I said.

He clasped a hand to each side of his head. "How many times do I have to tell you it doesn't matter?"

"Her name is Tina . . ."

*"Don't say anything more."* He was in my face, spitting saliva. *"I don't want to know her real name."*

"Ryan, she'd hidden her driver's license."

He stepped back. "She probably doesn't want her clients to know who she really is. She's just protecting herself."

"And she has gun."

"It's from Tiffany's, for God's sake."

"It can kill the same as any other gun."

"A client gave it to her in case she ever had a problem."

"Gee, why didn't I think of being a prostitute so I could use my clients as an excuse?"

"Did you take anything from her?"

"Of course not," I said, offended.

He glared. "You've gone too far this time. I'm calling Heath off the case."

"Please don't. I think my mother is alive."

He stared at me. "Christ, Diana, you don't even like her. Why would you want her to be alive?"

"And I think Tanya knows it too."

"Did you ever call your agent back?"

"What does that have to do with anything?"

"Did you?" he yelled at me.

"No!"

'This time you're the one who's fucking up. Not me."

"Ryan?"

"What?"

"Don't tell Tanya about this."

"Shit! You're relentless." He stomped out onto the deck and left.

I slumped on the sofa.

No. I wasn't okay.

The phone didn't ring all evening long. I'd hoped Rodriquez would call with information. Finally, just as I was crawling into bed, Heath phoned to tell me Ryan had taken him off the case.

"Diana, you can't go around breaking into my clients' houses."

"I broke into a friend's home."

"What possessed you?"

"Instinct. Opportunity. Did Rodriquez find out anything yet?"

"Tomorrow."

"Are you still going to work the case?"

His voice softened. "Don't worry. I won't walk away." He hung up.

I turned off the lights, turned on the TV and took my sleeping pill.

I waited for sleep. Nothing. I took a second pill and put the bottle back in the drawer. I was now taking two pills a night.

No, I wasn't okay.

Finally I slept the perfect drugged-out sleep, my unconscious frozen.

The pain was immediate. It started in my scalp. I tried to reach back to feel my head but I couldn't move. Someone was pulling my hair. I was dreaming. Having a nightmare. Wake up. Wake up. But I couldn't do that either. My head was pulled so far back that my mouth opened. And then I was choking. Fumes curled up into my nose. Brandy. Poured hot down my throat. I gulped and gulped and gagged. Pills filled my mouth. I tried to spit them out. My hair was yanked harder and harder. My neck bent back until I thought it would snap. More pills filled my mouth. I choked. Swallowed. Choked. Gasped. More booze. No air. My stomach heaved. No more breath. I gasped and gasped back into my dead dead dead sleep.

# CHAPTER FORTY

M y throat hurt like hell. I opened my eyes. I had a vague
recollection that I had accomplished this effort before.
Awakening, then sleeping. Nurses asking me to repeat
my name. Now I was wide awake and staring at the ceiling. Floating
voices in the air asked doctors and nurses to go to numbered sta-
tions. I peered around the room. A sad blue curtain was pulled
around my bed. A blood pressure band on my arm connected to
a monitor, tightened on its own then slowly released. I found it
comforting. A clamp on my index finger also was connected to the
monitor. An IV bag hung above me. What looked like its umbilical
cord snaked down to a needle inserted into the top of my hand.

In a chair next to my bed, Heath slept, his head tilted to one side,
lips apart, face unshaven, ashen.

"Hi," I croaked.

At the sound of my voice, he jerked upright, alert. "You're awake. How are you feeling?"

"Throat hurts."

"That's probably from the stomach pump."

I remembered the pain. Choking. Trying to get my breath. To swallow. To keep swallowing so I wouldn't suffocate and die. I grabbed his hand and winced, feeling the needle in mine. Tears welled in my eyes and ran down my temples and into my hair.

With his free hand he snapped a Kleenex out of a box on the table next to me. He dabbed at my eyes.

"I didn't do this to myself," I told him.

"I never thought you did. Don't cry."

"I'm pissed off."

"So am I."

"I keep remembering something, but not quite."

"Don't push it. It'll come back to you." He released my hand, pulled his chair closer. "It had to be someone who knew you took pills."

"Christ, I can't stop crying."

A hand pulled back the curtain, and a pudgy nurse approached the bed.

"How are you feeling?"

"Throat hurts."

Checking the monitors, she replied, "We had to pump your stomach. Are those tears of joy for being alive?"

"I don't know."

"Well, they should be. Just remember Marilyn Monroe never made it to the hospital."

"Marilyn Monroe? What hospital?" I asked.

"You're in St. John's in Santa Monica," Heath said.

"You're on the private floor," the nurse explained. "Under wraps. No press can get to you. Dr. Orvis will be in soon. Here." She handed me a stick with something cold on the end of it. "Suck on this. I'll get you some tea."

I stuck it in my mouth and looked at Heath. "Marilyn Monroe?"

"They think you had an accidental overdose."

"I want to go home."

"Diana . . ."

The doctor swept in, his white coat flaring with authority. "I'm Dr. Orvis. How are you feeling?"

"Throat hurts."

"I'm not surprised. Other than that, how are you feeling?"

"Fine."

His gray eyes narrowed.

"Okay. Like I have a major hangover."

"We can give you something for that."

"More pills?"

He didn't find that amusing.

"I am going to have a psychiatrist see you," he said. "And I want to keep you overnight for observation. I'm going to raise your bed now." He pushed something and the head went slowly up until I was in a sitting position. "You feel dizzy?"

"No."

"You seem to have come through this quite well. At least this time." He used his stethoscope to listen to my heart. Told me to breathe in and out. Looked into my eyes with a small light. "How many sleeping pills do you normally take a night?"

"One." Oh, hell. "Sometimes two."

"You're going to break that habit, aren't you?"

I nodded. He studied the monitor. "Good thing your neighbor found you. Nice to see you awake." He turned and left the room.

"Neighbor?" I looked at Heath.

Ryan poked his head in the door. "The doctor said it was okay to come in."

I smiled at him. "You saved me."

Tanya walked in behind him.

"Not me," Ryan said. "Tanya did."

Surprised, I looked at her.

"I was coming back to Ryan's last night," she said, "I noticed your deck door was open. All the lights in your house were out. I got one of those funny feelings. You know what I mean?"

"No."

"I found you sprawled on your bed. Lucky for you, you vomited up most of the pills," she explained matter-of-factly.

"She called 911 then came and got me. I called Heath." Ryan moved to the bed, gently turned my hand over, and placed a key in it.

I stared at it. It was his house key.

"I'm sorry," he said.

"Oh, Ryan, I didn't try to kill myself."

"What do you mean?" he asked.

"She means someone tried to kill her, baby," Tanya said.

"I'd like to speak to Tanya alone," I said.

"We'll be right outside." Heath guided a confused Ryan out of the room.

"You're Tina Andres. Not Tanya."

"Everybody is somebody else in Hollywood. Or wants to be. If your PI is running a check on me, he won't find anything."

"Aren't you going to ask how I know your real name?"

"Who says it's my real name?"

"Sheriff Ford says you're dangerous." My body tensed as I said his name. A memory flickered. I couldn't grab hold of it.

She snorted. "Yeah, right. So dangerous I saved your ass. He doesn't like girls like me on his beach."

And then I remembered Ford standing in my bedroom, opening the nightstand drawer to retrieve Gerard Quincy's gun and spotting my vial of pills. I felt myself pale.

"You okay?" she asked, concerned.

"Throat hurts."

"You need rest." She started to leave.

"Wait. I know it was my mother in that limo at Starbucks. That means you were with her. You know she's alive."

"The pills have jumbled your brain. I told you that woman was a client."

"Don't harm her. Or . . ."

"Or what?"

"I'll come after you."

"What a world we live in. I save your life and you threaten mine. Doesn't seem fair somehow." She flipped her hair over her shoulder in a fuck-you gesture and walked out of the room.

I closed my eyes, trying to gather strength. Then I threw back the covers, swung my legs over the side, and sat on the edge of the bed, letting the world right itself. I took a deep breath and pulled out my IV. Blood bubbled at the spot of the puncture. The room swayed. Heath came back in. When he realized what I'd done, he grabbed another Kleenex and pressed it on my hand where the needle had been.

"I want to go home."

"You will. Keep pressure on that," he said.

"Sheriff Ford. He knew I was taking pills. He saw them in the drawer of my nightstand when he was getting Quincy's gun. He warned me about all the accidental suicides he'd seen. It sounded like a threat at the time. It worried me."

"What's his connection to your mother?

My mind was muddled. "I don't know. I need my clothes."

"You don't have any clothes here. Concentrate, Diana. Why would Ford want you dead?"

"He's close with Marc Decker. I think they were trying to make Quincy's murder look like a suicide. Maybe to protect StarView from bad publicity or something."

"So Ford is doing StarView's bidding?"

"Maybe he planted the Glock at the scene of Quincy's death."

"He didn't know you had Quincy's gun?"

"I caught him in a lie."

I swung my legs over the side of the bed, took a deep breath, and stood. Leaning on the bedside table, I said, "Decker was there when Ford asked me to ID Quincy." I started to remove the clamp on my finger.

Heath stopped me. "You're wired. Remove that, and the entire staff will be in here. Sit down and don't do anything."

I sat on the bed again. "Ford's the only one who knew I took sleeping pills. He saw them, Heath, he saw them."

He was studying the monitors. He hit some buttons. All right." He removed the clamp and the blood pressure wrap.

"I want to get the son of a bitch."

"We will. I've been thinking while you've been talking. I may even have a plan, if you're physically up for it."

"I am." I stood and headed for the door.

"Diana, you can't leave with your ass hanging out. As beautiful as it is."

He opened a cupboard and took out a clean gown and put it on me like a coat so my backside was covered.

The nurse walked in with a plastic cup of tea. "What's all this?" she demanded. "And who turned the monitors off?" She slammed the tea down on the table. It sloshed over.

"I'm driving her home." Heath took off his jacket and put it on me.

I felt his warmth and leaned into him.

"The doctor's instructions are that you spend the night," she ordered. "He hasn't released you."

"I'm releasing myself."

"You'll be back," she warned.

"No, I won't."

# CHAPTER FORTY-ONE

stared at my vomit, spread over the bed and onto the floor. A
stale sour smell permeated the room. My struggle for life. I leaned
against the doorjamb. Heath walked in and opened the window.
Then he grabbed my cell off the nightstand and handed it to me.

"Call Ford," he said.

"What if he won't come here?"

"He will."

I phoned him. With Heath watching, I told Ford that I was afraid.
That I knew someone had tried to kill me and I wasn't suicidal. I
needed to talk to him right away at home, where I was resting. He
said he'd be here in about an hour.

I disconnected. "An hour."

Heath checked his watch. "It's five fifteen now."

"I have to shower." I took off his jacket and gave it back to him. Then I got clothes from my closet and dresser and went into the bathroom.

Forty-five minutes later, I was propped up against pillows on the sofa and trying to eat toast and sip coffee Heath had made for me.

He was leaning against the fireplace. "You remember what you're going to say to him?"

"I'm an actress. I won't forget my lines."

"I'll be on the deck. Against the side of the house. You won't see me unless Ford starts something. When he leaves, I'll take the walkway out to PCH and follow him in my car. Don't expect him to confess. The point is for me to tail him. See if takes me to someone who he's working with. You going to be all right alone?"

I nodded.

"Eat some more toast." He rubbed the bump on his nose.

I dipped a piece in my coffee and took a bite. "You falling in love with me, Heath?"

"What made you say that?"

"Instinct." The doorbell rang. "He's early."

"He's scared." He slipped out onto the deck, leaving the door open. Soon he was out of sight.

I got up and answered the door.

My heartbeat was picking up speed as I ushered Ford into the living room. I sat back down on the sofa. Ford was as pale as I was, and the bags under his eyes were thicker and darker. He sat in the new chair. His leather belt and holster creaked like an old man's bones.

"How are you feeling?" he asked.

"Throat hurts."

"Stomach pump. I read the report my officers made on the scene. They didn't see evidence of another person involved. The doctors are calling it an accidental overdose."

"You and I know that's not true."

His chin lifted. "How do we know that?"

"Because I'm not suicidal. And you were the only person outside my friends who knew I took sleeping pills."

"What are you saying?"

"I think you tried to kill me." My body tensed, waiting for his reaction.

"Now, why would I do that?" His eyes were hard on me. His voice was casual.

"Maybe because I know that Gerard Quincy didn't kill himself. Someone murdered him. And you're trying to cover it up."

"Why would I want to risk anything for Gerard Quincy?"

"Because he knew about my mother's scorpion bracelet. In fact, he wanted it. At least, that's what he told me. I think he thought he could use it to keep himself from being killed. I'm also sure he knew what Elizabeth Rodgers knew."

"Yeah? What's that?"

"My mother is alive."

He ran his hand through his gray-blond hair. "Are you sure you're all right? Didn't lose some oxygen to the brain?"

Anger flared. "You're a dirty cop."

He shot to his feet. His hand rested on the butt of his holstered gun. "How the hell was I supposed to know you had Quincy's gun? We found a Glock near his body, and I didn't plant it."

"How much is Decker paying you to pick up his trash?"

"Decker?" In one long stride he was leaning over me, his lips thin and colorless. I could smell his sweat. "I'm a deputy sheriff. Nobody is going to believe anything a half-baked actress who tried to kill herself says. I'll make sure of that."

He rose up and strode out of the room. I heard the front door slam shut. I sat for moment, letting my adrenaline spin out of control. Then I got up and went out on the deck.

Heath was gone. I gripped the railing and gazed out at the ocean. I breathed it in. My tears were back. It was so good to see the goddamn ocean.

Wiping my wet cheeks, I realized I couldn't stand around waiting for Heath to show up or call. I needed to do something. I moved back inside and locked the French doors. Then I went into my room and pulled the duvet off the bed, trying not to breathe the foul odor. Gathering it up, I noticed something flutter to the floor. At first I thought it was down, then I looked closer. It was a white feather with a wooden bead attached. Crouching, I picked it up. My adrenaline was back at full speed. The StarView attendants wore necklaces of wooden beads and a feather. Eddie had told us it meant hope. My skin turned clammy.

I hurried down the hallway to get my cell from the coffee table to call Heath. To tell him I'd been mistaken. Eddie stood in the middle of the room smiling as he always did when he greeted me at StarView. I stopped, the feather clutched in my fist.

"How did you get in here?" I asked, trying to keep my voice even.

"You left your front door unlocked. I was sitting out there in a van when the sheriff arrived and left mad as hell. Then I saw Heath get into his car and follow him. So what the hell are you doing alive?"

My heart was pounding. I thought about telling him that Tanya had found me, but something made me stop. "I managed to wake up enough to hit 911 on my phone. I guess I mumbled until I passed out again. That's what the EMT's told me. I don't remember it."

His pool boy face toughened. "Give me the goddamn feather."

Don't let your voice go high, Diana. "What feather?"

"I saw you pick it up off the floor. It's in your hand." He gestured toward my fist. "You going to take me on?" He reached under his shirt, pulled out a pistol, and aimed it at me. "Oh, look what I found. A gun."

"You can't shoot me. It'd be too tough to explain. Fuck, I feel light-headed." I swayed. Let my body go limp.

He rushed me and grabbed for my fist. I kneed him in the crotch. Hard. Grunting, he staggered back, gun hand dropping. I whirled around and grabbed the lamp off the side table. The feather fell from my hand as I tore the cord out of the socket and slammed the lamp into his face. He let go of the gun as he went down on his side. Groaning and wallowing, he tried to hold his balls and his head at the same time.

I snapped up his weapon from where he'd dropped it and trained it on him. "I should shoot you. You almost killed me, you bastard."

From behind me, a muscular arm wrapped around my neck like a cobra and squeezed my windpipe. The pistol slipped from my hand. I clawed at the arm. A black hood jerked down over my head.

# CHAPTER FORTY-TWO

M y hands were tied behind my back with plastic cuffs so tightly they bit into my wrists. I was shoved hard into some kind of vehicle and landed facedown on a carpeted floor that reeked of oil. The black hood clung to my face when I breathed in. I twisted my face away from the carpet. Even through the hood, the stench of oil was nauseating.

As the passenger and driver doors opened and banged shut, the Arm, as I'd come to think of him, chewed out Eddie for being a useless fuckhead. The engine roared to life and we were moving. I listened for sounds that I might recognize, but the vehicle— a van, I thought—rattled loudly, and my head and heart were hammering.

As the van sped around a corner, I rolled back and forth like something forgotten in the trunk of your car. Something you never remembered to take out. When it turned again I bent my knees, trying use my feet to keep from hitting the side panels. Blind, I couldn't judge when the turns were coming. Is this what the perps meant by taking a "wild ride"? I couldn't get away from the stink of oil.

The sharp edges of the plastic bracelets dug deeper into my flesh. Focus, Diana. Closing my eyes against the pain and the violently rocking van, I made myself think about Eddie and decided he didn't have the sense to kill me on his own. Somebody had to be behind it. Decker? But why? I wasn't harming StarView. Walford? It always came back to him. The Healer.

We'd been driving for a very long time.

I thought of Heath. At some point, he'd come back to my house, but would he see the feather with the wood bead attached to it that I'd dropped somewhere? I knew he'd remember what the feather and bead meant. If he saw it.

Suddenly the van stopped, projecting my body forward. My head hit a metal partition. Shit. Already weak, I didn't know if I could take much more. Then I heard the engine turn off. My survival instinct kicked in.

All my senses grew alert.

The van's doors opened and closed.

"I'll get her out. Did you get that fucking feather?" the Arm growled at Eddie.

"I found it on the floor. No problem."

Now I knew there was no hope of rescue. There was no way Heath could find me now.

"Right. No problem. I come in and you're lying on your side grabbing at your balls. Go take up your security post."

*Think*, Diana, *think*. The only part of my body I could use was my legs.

"Hey, Blondie," the Arm said.

As irritating as his calling me that was, I didn't move.

"Hey! Sit up. Scoot on down here."

Still. Absolutely still. It's easier to play dead with a hood over you.

"Hey! *Shit*. You gonna make me come in there after you?" The van shifted under the Arm's weight. He was crawling in with me.

I readied myself, but I could only sense where he was. His clothes brushed against my arms. Before I could kick or raise my knee, his forearm pressed down on my windpipe.

"I'm not as easy as Eddie," he warned. "You gonna come with me nicely?"

I managed a strangled, "Yes."

Keeping his arm on my throat, he used his free hand to jerk off my hood. We blinked at each other. He was on my right side leaning over me. He had the face of an accountant. Unremarkable. Thin wire-frame glasses perched on his pinkish nose. His hair was light gray and thinning. But his eyes were a little too close. A little too uncaring.

Taking a gun from his jacket pocket, he aimed it at me as he moved backward out of the van. I sat up, edged forward. As my feet touched the ground, I saw I was in a garage. Gray painted walls. Gray cement floor. The van was parked next to a black limo. And I thought of my mother.

I cleared my throat. "Do you drive that?"

"I don't have a chauffeur's license." A stickler for the law. Maybe he *was* an accountant.

Grabbing my shoulder, he shoved me toward a door painted the same gray as the walls and pressed his palm over some kind of identification detector. The door slid open. We entered an ordinary laundry room.

"Somehow I expected more."

"Washer and dryer are top of the line."

He went through the same ID process with the laundry room door.

We arrived in a large designer kitchen. A chef in a white cook's jacket hovered over a Viking stove. The air smelled of sautéing chanterelle mushrooms.

Tanya sat at a white quartz counter on a barstool, all long legs and silky black hair, black jeans, motorcycle boots, and black leather jacket. She was eating a carrot.

"Why am I not surprised?" I said.

Ignoring me, she stared at the Arm and ordered, "Put the weapon away, tough guy. Diana can't go anywhere. We're locked down tight."

"You didn't see her in action." The Arm slipped the gun back into his pocket and pushed me toward another door.

"What the hell is wrong with you?" Tanya demanded. "You can't take her in there with cuffs on."

"I don't have anything to cut them off with."

"We're in a kitchen. Find some scissors, idiot. She looks like hell."

"Not my fault," the Arm grumbled as he opened and closed drawers.

The chef ignored everyone, delicately tasting a chanterelle.

Tanya reached into her orange leather bag. I froze. For a moment I thought she was going to come out with the Tiffany gun. Instead she held a lipstick. Moving close to me, she pulled off the top, nudged her index finger under my chin, and tilted my chin up.

"Relax." She applied the lipstick. Creamy smooth. Under her breath she said, "Do what *he* says." Then she spoke louder. "Press your lips together. There, you look great." She fluffed my hair. I jerked my head away from her hands.

Who was she talking about?

The Arm now held a pair of very long and pointed scissors. He moved behind me. I felt the long blades cold against my skin. *Snip. Snip.* My arms fell to my sides. I wanted to rub my wrists. But I couldn't lift them. Tanya did it for me.

"Feel better?" she asked. Then she looked down and saw the raw impressions on my skin. She glared at the Arm. "Jerk! Look what you did to her!"

My wrists tingled with my blood beginning to circulate. What game was she playing? I stared at her with venom.

"Shut the fuck up, *Tanya*," he grumbled. He clamped down on my shoulder and we headed toward another door. A swinging one with no ID required.

Now I was in a cozy living room. By a stone fireplace, two white-linen, slipcovered sofas with blue-and-white pillows plumped on them faced each other. A distressed wood coffee table sat between. Near the fireplace was a staircase. The Arm disappeared back into the kitchen.

The coziness of the room diminished when I saw steel shutters covering the windows. Across the room was a row of French doors through which light poured in. No shutters there. I moved to them and peered out.

My mother sat on the edge of a lounge by a small pool. Still beautiful. Still glamorous. She wore white jeans and a black sweater. Gold sandals shimmered on her feet. Her blond hair was longer. Her studious thick black-framed glasses were incongruous yet fitting. "They're a touch of reality," she had once said. Walford sat across from her, holding her hand. They leaned in toward each other, talking. My heart tilted.

My mother *was* alive.

I tried to open the doors, but they wouldn't budge. I pounded on the panes of glass. They were thick, some kind of strange material. Despite all my efforts, I couldn't make a sound to get her attention. I watched her tip her head down. Her long blond hair fell forward. I breathed heavily. All the betrayals and anger vanished. I was a daughter who wanted to embrace her mother.

# CHAPTER FORTY-THREE

Hearing footsteps on the stairs, I whirled around. Marc Decker was coming down, oxford shoes gleaming, hair perfect. He wore an Italian sport jacket that adored him, and gray slacks. He crossed the room, and stopped next to me. His teal-blue eyes peered down his patrician nose at me as he gestured through the glass at my mother and Walford.

"They're deeply in love," he said.

"I want to see her."

He brought an elegant hand to his chin, his college ring flashing ruby-red.

"First, I have a business proposition. Come and sit down."

"No, I want to see her. *Now.*"

"You don't seem to understand the precariousness of your situation. Here, you're no different than one of our addicts. But instead of being controlled by alcohol or drugs, you're controlled by me. Just like your mother. Just like Walford."

The sun had set. A gray-and-lavender afterglow streaked across my mother and Walford and the high metal security fence that surrounded them. Was she crying? I remembered how Walford had been sitting beside a pool talking to a crying StarView patient when I first saw him. I pressed my hands on the windowpanes. A man near them leaned against a tree, watching. He had a bald head like the limo driver I'd seen.

I turned on Decker. "You've kidnapped my mother and Dr. Walford?"

"Well, let's say I found them a very safe place to live. It's nice, isn't it?" he asked, looking around with pride.

"But you let Walford out on his own."

"He's allowed to see his private patients, but he's hardly a free agent. StarView couldn't go on without him, so if he tried to tell anyone of his predicament, your mother would have to be killed. Pity. And he couldn't live with that. After all, he was the one who started all this."

"What do you mean?" I asked sharply.

"He abducted her and then conspired to create a fake death certificate. It does make one wonder who kidnapped whom, doesn't it?" He grinned. Taking his cell from his pocket, he tapped it a few times. A metal shade concealed behind a ceiling beam slowly rattled down, covering the French doors and the view of my mother. I sucked in my breath. I was in a steel cage. But so was Decker.

I was furious and afraid for her. "You tried to have me killed, and my mother is your prisoner. Why should I discuss anything with you?" I demanded.

"I'd think those two facts should be reason enough." He moved to one of the sofas and sat. He gestured for me to sit opposite him.

I did, but slowly.

"Here's my proposition. I'll let you go, and in return you'll never mention this to anyone. You'll stop your irritating amateur sleuthing and get on with your life being the actress and daughter of the famous but dead Nora Poole."

"That's it?"

"I'm asking you to live a lie. And for that StarView remains one of the top rehab centers in the world and Nora Poole gets to live with the man she loves. Oh, and I'd like her bracelet back."

"You broke into my house with my mother?"

"No, my chauffeur Milo was with Nora. She said she knew where you'd keep such a thing. But of course it wasn't there. Milo verified that."

I thought of the photograph she'd left out for me to see. "Why is the scorpion so important now?"

"A loose end. That's all. I don't like them." Crossing one leg over the other, he rested his arm along the back of his sofa. "Nora said it fell off her wrist. I didn't believe her, of course. Elizabeth Rodgers and Gerard Quincy found it on one of their walks."

My mother was near or hidden in StarView, I thought. But that's not where I was now. It'd taken the Arm a long time to get me here.

"Gerard stupidly blurted out who it belonged to, and that he'd seen Nora Poole. Elizabeth wouldn't give it back. She hoarded that scorpion like a starving person hoards a piece of bread. She wanted to give it to her daughter, that actress, I can't think of her name."

"Gabrielle Hays. You're paying her a great deal of money for the death of her mother. I'd think you'd remember her name."

Ignoring me, he continued. "In her alcohol-marinated mind, Elizabeth thought Ms. Hays would give it to you. She was having dinner with her daughter that night. But I couldn't let that happen. I went to see her to get the damn scorpion back. Elizabeth ran."

"You were driving the Range Rover with Quincy. It *was* you she was afraid of."

He shrugged. "I had no idea my mere presence would make her act so recklessly."

"You mean force her to kill herself."

"So many suicides. Forced. Attempted." His long fingers drummed impatiently on the sofa.

"Mine wasn't a suicide."

"No, Eddie tried to kill you and failed."

"How did you know I took pills?"

"My helpful idiot Deputy Sheriff Ford told me. *En passant.*" He took his cell out of his pocket again and tapped on it. "I'd like to see Eddie, Tanya, and William," he said, then disconnected.

In moments the three of them came through the swinging kitchen door and stood in a line at the end of the coffee table.

"You've met William. He brought you here."

William, the Arm, adjusted his glasses.

"And you know Tanya well. Your mother is very close to her. And of course so is Ryan Johns. Your mother and Tanya take limousine rides together. It gets Nora out of the house."

My stomach tightened.

"Tanya has a difficult job," Decker continued. "But she handles it with grace and beauty. She's what I think is called a plant, a spy. She'll remain with Ryan while you go on with your life."

Tanya stared straight ahead, never looking at either of us.

"In other words," I said, "she'll be spying on Ryan and me for you."

"Yes. But now that you know, maybe you'll grow as fond of her as Nora has."

"You really think I would live that way? That I would let Ryan?"

Decker's gaze fell on Eddie, who stood with his hand in pockets waiting to hear his job description.

Instead Decker asked, "Eddie, who is this sitting on the sofa across from me?"

Eddie was startled by the question. "Diana Poole."

"Why is she sitting on the sofa?"

"You asked William and me to bring her here."

"No, she's here because she's alive." He sighed. "I hate incompetence, especially when it's mixed with stupidity." He leaned over and opened a drawer in the coffee table. Taking out a pistol, he swung it toward Eddie and shot him in the middle of his forehead.

The Arm lurched sideways. Tanya paled, but never moved or broke her stare. I jumped to my feet, hands over my mouth. Eddie stood a moment staring at Decker, then he collapsed. There was little blood on his forehead. Just a round hole with a red trickle running down the bridge of his nose. But the back of his head was leaking brain and bone.

Decker smiled at me. "Yes, I think you and Ryan can live *that* way. I'll walk Miss Poole out," he told Tanya and the Arm. "You'll take care of Eddie." He slipped the gun inside his jacket and moved toward me.

Stunned, I let him take me by the elbow and guide me out of the room and into the kitchen. All I could think about was that this evil, crazy man planned to dominate the rest our lives. Not if I could help it.

"Dinner will be ready soon," the chef told him, seemingly oblivious to the gunshot he must've heard. It was as if he lived inside of *bon appétit* magazine.

"Thanks, Charles. Tell Ms. Poole and Dr. Walford." He swept the hood off the counter, opened a drawer, and took out a fresh pair of plastic cuffs. He pressed his palm against the ID detector on the wall, and the door to the laundry room swung open. He repeated the process, and we were in the dark garage. My hands began to tremble.

He flipped a light on. "Don't waste your time screaming, Diana. It's soundproof. Do we see eye to eye?"

"Yes. My mother and I can only stay alive by living under your violent, insane rules."

He blinked. "That's one way to look at it. But I see it as win-win for everybody. Your mother is with the man she loves, and he's with her. StarView continues on, doing good for its patients. And you'll have your life back. I'll give you twenty-four hours to get the scorpion."

"What do I do with it when I have it?"

"I'll call you. I'm afraid you'll have to wear these again. I'll make the cuffs looser." He turned me around.

I forced myself to stop shaking as he fastened the bracelets around my sore wrists.

"You must know the kidnapper is just as much a hostage as those he takes," I told him.

He ignored me. "You'll be riding in the limo. Eddie will be in the van. I want you to remember Eddie. Remember how I 'reward' incompetence."

He opened the limo's rear door. Then he slipped the hood over my head and helped me into the backseat like a perfect gentleman. "Don't forget," he said, leaning in. "Your mother is already dead. If she dies again, her blood will be on your hands. Not mine." He closed the door.

Waiting for the driver, I sat in silence. In darkness. Listening to my pounding heart. Even through the black hood I could smell the soft scent of my mother's perfume.

# CHAPTER FORTY-FOUR

Sometime later the limo dropped me off about four blocks from my house. Milo, the driver, removed my cuffs and hood and yanked me out the door.

"Your mother is a pain in the ass."

"So am I."

He drove off.

I began to walk.

Cars raced by. Headlights flashed over me, at times blinding me. The traffic was heavy. Why didn't he drop me off at my house, I wondered. That was the least of my worries. I walked faster. I was cold and exhausted. My anger, my fear for my mother fueled me. I began to jog. Did Decker really think if I gave him the scorpion bracelet he wouldn't kill me? I wasn't Eddie. A chill ran though me. Maybe I was.

Near my house I stopped dead. Breathing hard, I squinted into the traffic. A limo, its turn signal blinking, was waiting in line at a red light. Waiting to turn left off the highway onto Windswept Road, which led to StarView. That's why Milo dropped me a few blocks away. He didn't want me to see where he was going

As I ran to my house, the front door flew open. Heath bolted out. Rodriquez was right behind him.

"Are you all right?" Heath shouted. "I was crazy with worry."

"Get in the car!" I rushed toward his Escalade.

Heath and Rodriquez stared at each other.

"Now!" I yelled.

Rodriquez slammed the front door shut. The goofy dolphins watched as we piled into Heath's car. Rodriquez got into the backseat and leaned forward.

"Where are we going?" Heath pulled out onto PCH, tires screeching.

"Windswept Road. I was kidnapped. I thought the house where they took me was far away. But I couldn't tell. I had a hood over my head."

"Hood? Cool," Rodriquez said.

"Who kidnapped you? What in hell happened?" Heath demanded as he raced the car in and out of traffic.

"Decker."

"Shit. We're going to StarView?"

He caught the green light at Windswept and made a sharp left. I pressed my hands against the dashboard as oncoming cars honked and skidded to brake. Balancing, Rodriquez held onto the back of the seat.

"No. Slow down. Turn off your lights."

Heath slowed and turned off his lights. "What exactly are we looking for, Diana?"

I watched all around as we floated along in the darkness past the empty ghostly houses. "A limo and a house. A safe house. Heavy security. Metal shutters on the front windows. They all look the same. My mother and Walford are in one of them."

"You found her?" Heath said.

"Decker killed Eddie. Shot him in the head because he didn't succeed in killing me." I looked at Heath. "It wasn't Ford."

"I know. He and I had a little talk. Turns out he's on the take from Decker to promote StarView in the community. But that's as far as his dirty cop goes."

"They're all the same, man," Rodriquez muttered.

"Decker is holding them prisoner. The house would have to stand out."

"If it's a safe house, it wouldn't look any different than the others," Heath said.

"But it has metal shutters over the front windows."

"Fake façade," Rodriquez said. "Is that redundant?"

"I thought they were miles away. They were just driving around to confuse me. They were here all the time."

"We'll find her, Diana," Heath said.

We were at the top of the road. StarView loomed up in the darkness. The gates were closed. Low garden lights glowed dimly along the paths and stairs, casting an otherworldly glow on the main structure.

"We could check each house," Rodriquez said.

"I have a better idea," Heath said. "Barrie Singer."

"Who?" Rodriquez asked.

"The only person who still owns a house here."

"The one-woman Greek chorus," I said.

"She has to know something." Heath drove around the curve of the cul-de-sac and pulled into Barrie Singer's driveway.

The three of us got out of the car. Heath knocked on her door. After a few moments, a light turned on inside. He knocked again.

"Who is it?" she barked through the front door.

"It's Leo Heath. Do you remember me?"

"And Diana Poole," I said.

"I'm in bed."

"We need your help," I tried. "My mother's life is at stake."

"Your mother's dead."

"No, she's not."

The porch light went on. Heath reached up inside the lantern and twisted the bulb out and tossed it in the hedges.

The door opened a crack. "What happened to my light?"

"It must be out," I said.

"Did you say Nora Poole is alive?"

"Yes."

"Oh, thank God." She released the chain. "I thought I was going nuts. Or StarView was playing tricks on me."

"They play tricks on you?" Heath asked.

"They bully me. They want my house. I thought they were trying something new, like driving me crazy." She clutched a bathrobe to her bony body. "Come in the living room. I'll make us coffee."

"We don't have time." All I could think of was how Decker shot Eddie.

As we went inside, she left through a swinging door. I looked around. The room was the exact replica of Decker's living room but sparsely decorated.

"It's the same layout as Decker's," I told Heath.

Soon Barrie returned with a tray holding gold-trimmed china coffee cups and saucers. They looked like an old wedding gift. Then I remembered her husband had left her because she wouldn't sell her house.

"They're all the same. Contractor built."

Heath nodded to Rodriquez, who strolled off, scouting the house.

"Where's he going?"

Heath took the tray from her and set it down.

I was ready to jump out of my skin. "Tell us what you saw," I snapped at her.

That angry, bitter look came over her face.

"She's very worried about her mother," Heath explained gently.

"Well, you should be," she spoke as if were my fault.

Rodriquez was coming down the stairs.

"A limo was backing out of the garage," Barrie said.

"Which garage?" Heath asked.

She hurried to her window and pulled back the drapes and pointed across the street. "Sixth house down. It's hard to see without streetlights." She let the drapes fall back. "I saw a blond woman . . ."

We were already on our way out of the house.

Heath opened the back of his car and unlocked a compartment in the floorboard. Inside was a cache of weapons. "How many are in the house, Diana?"

"Is that legal?"

"Diana."

"William. Milo. Tanya. All are armed, I think. I'm not sure which side Tanya is on, but I don't trust her. Plus there's Charles, the chef. I think he just cooks. And my mother, Walford, and Decker. Decker has a gun. There might be others."

Rodriquez took out a long rifle and a Glock pistol. I saw a rope. I reached in and took it. "There's a very tall steel fence in back with overgrown bushes."

"Neat. I love to rappel." Rodriquez took it.

"Something else. All the doors are locked. The only way you can get in is by your palm print. I saw the Arm, that's William, use it. He has gray thinning hair and wears wire glasses."

Rodriquez searched around and came out with electrical clippers. He looked at Heath. "You just taking your Colt?"

Heath nodded, then chose an S&W pistol and handed it to me. "I need you to stay here and keep watch, Diana." He closed the compartment, locked it, and handed me the keys.

"No, Heath."

He gave me a hard look. "We may need to get out of here fast. Be ready. We'll put our cells on vibrate. Call if you see anything. Anything at all."

They darted across the street and disappeared into the shadows along the houses. It wasn't until then I realized I didn't have my phone.

I'd been leaning against the Escalade, worrying, for about five minutes when the garage door of the safe house opened and the limo, its lights out, rear end fishtailing in the moonlight, backed out, swerved, and careened down the street.

I leaped into the Escalade, jammed the key into the ignition, and turned on the engine. The car revved powerfully under me. I backed out of the driveway, spun it around, and sped down Windswept Road.

# CHAPTER FORTY-FIVE

kept right behind the limousine as it sped north on PCH. The driver was erratic and reckless, which led me to believe it wasn't Milo driving. I flashed my lights and saw Decker behind the wheel. Someone was slumped in the front passenger seat. My mother was in the backseat.

I closed in as we sped past Starbucks and through Zuma Beach. The limo was going much too fast, veering into oncoming lanes, swinging back. Passing cars honked. The limo's tires squealed and in an abrupt side-to-side motion it swerved off the highway. Decker had lost control. The long vehicle plunged into brush.

I slowed but stayed with him. The Escalade bumped and bucked. Dirt and sand billowed up from the limo's tires. Suddenly it fish-tailed down the hillside, and I hit the brakes. Turning off the ignition, I grabbed the S&W, leaped out of the car, and ran frantically after it.

Breathing hard, I stood at the edge of the hill, watching the vehicle careen down, bouncing off rocks, shredding small trees. The brake light lit up as it headed toward the edge of what looked like a sheer cliff. Its nose tipped dangerously down toward the whitecaps on the black ocean below. I scrambled down the hill.

The driver's door flew open. I could hear my mother screaming and swearing. Decker got out with a briefcase in his hand. He looked dazed.

"Stop!" I yelled, holding my gun on him.

Dropping the briefcase, he whirled around and reached into his coat pocket and came out with his gun.

I fired and missed him. *Shit.*

As he aimed at me, I fired again. Nothing happened. The damn thing had jammed.

"Kill him! Kill him!" Tanya screamed as she reeled out of the limo.

I could see my mother crawling over the front seat. "Get my mother out!"

The car teetered. Tanya yanked her out by the shoulders, then supported her so she didn't fall.

At the same time, Decker was walking toward me. Even in the moonlight I could see how dark his face was with rage.

I raised the gun again. *Click.*

Decker stood in front of me, his pistol aimed at my belly. "You and Nora Poole have ruined my life." The man's eyes were wild.

"Decker!" Tanya yelled, then bent down to her boot.

He turned. I slammed the butt of my gun into the back of his head. Swaying, he pitched around and aimed his weapon at me again.

Tanya rose up. The gun exploded. I staggered backward.

Mother screamed, "No!"

Decker fell to the ground. Dirt and dust rose up around him, then settled on his elegant clothes. He stared up at me. He mouthed one word. *Bitch.* Then I stared at Tanya, who was standing, legs apart, the gun she'd fired still aimed in my direction. Then she smiled and dropped her arms.

"Diana!" Mother ran toward me and threw her arms around me. She hugged me tightly. All my mixed feelings roiled inside of me. But I didn't care. I was alive. *She* was alive. I held her tightly. Then we let go and stared at our reflections in each other's face.

Tanya joined us, holding her Tiffany gun in one hand and the briefcase in the other. "You missed your first shot. You need to go to the practice range." A bruise was forming on her perfect chin.

"I'm an actress. What do you want? What happened to you?"

"When your boys dismantled the ID detectors and broke in taking Decker's guys down, he grabbed Nora and shoved her into the limo."

"Then she leaped in. Trying to save me. They struggled, and he coldcocked her." Nora gently touched Tanya's bruise. Tanya stepped back. Not from pain, but the human touch.

"The bastard," she said. "Didn't know he had it in him."

"What's in there?" I gestured at the case in her hand.

"Decker's cash. About a hundred thousand. I'll count it later."

"Who are you really?" I asked her.

"As Decker said, he hired me to spy on you and Ryan and guard your mother."

"Do we have to stand here talking over a corpse? I feel like I'm in a Shakespeare play." Mother tossed her hair out of her face and straightened her lopsided glasses. "I want to get back and see if Sam is okay."

Thinking of Heath and Rodriquez, I said, "I'm sure he's safe."

A loud *crack* rocked us. We looked around as the side of the cliff broke, then crumbled, and the limousine flipped up, then over, and somersaulted down into the ocean.

"Thank God. I never want to ride in another fucking limo for the rest of my life," Mother announced. She stalked up the hill, her gold sandals shimmering.

At the Escalade, Tanya used her jacket to wipe down her gun.

"Thank you for saving me and Diana," Mother said.

"I didn't save anybody. And I didn't kill Decker," she spoke matter-of-factly.

Tanya took my hand and slapped the gun down on my palm. Then she pressed my fingers around the butt.

"What are you doing?" I asked.

"And I wasn't here. You shot Decker."

"What?"

"Saving your mother. Think about it. Your mother and Walford are going to go to jail. She let him kidnap her."

I stared at my mother. "You what?"

"I went with him willingly. I wanted to be out of this world but not. He just wanted to help me."

"I don't believe this."

"I never loved anybody like I love him."

"Love is no excuse." Christ, my life with my mother was beginning. Again.

"I hear Patel has gone back to India. Maybe it was Decker who forced him to make out a fake death certificate," Tanya offered.

"Patel was helping small children, for God's sake." I glared at my mother.

"He's not in India," she retorted. "The last time he talked to Patel Sam told him to hide out at Miss Bell's."

"What?"

"You're two creative women. You'll work it out." Swinging the briefcase, Tanya strode up to the highway.

"Wait a minute." I hurried after her. "You can't just walk away with all that cash."

"Yes. I can. Unless you're going to shoot me." She smiled. The passing cars illuminated her beautiful almond-shaped eyes. "Tell Ryan I'm sorry. I just couldn't give it up."

"Give up what?"

"The game."

"I don't know many hookers who shoot like you do."

"You don't know many hookers."

"He loves you."

"They all say that."

"No, they don't. Not Ryan."

Facing the oncoming cars, she held her up thumb. "I like him, Diana. More than any man I have before. But that's not saying much." Two cars sped by. The third one skidded to a stop. She opened the door, got in, and was gone.

For the rest of my life I would look back on that moment as the beginning of my new career. It was based on a big lie and a Tiffany blue gun.

# CHAPTER FORTY-SIX

Two weeks later I stood on my deck with my back to the ocean, looking through my open doors into the living room. On the sofa, my mother was laughing with Ryan. Near the fireplace, Rodriquez stood talking intensely with Sam, as I call Walford now.

I'd lied to the police, and I have no regrets. I know Mother doesn't.

We'd told Ford that Decker had kidnapped her. That he'd been obsessed with her. When Walford found out, he'd threatened to leave StarView and tell the police. Decker imprisoned him, saying he'd kill Nora Poole if Walford said anything. Personally, I wouldn't have believed it, but Ford was ready to accept anything we said as long as we didn't talk about the payoffs he'd been taking from Star-View. The FBI came in and sniffed around. That was a rough couple of days, but they'd had bigger criminals to fry and left.

My mother's "resurrection" was the hottest story. She made all the big TV shows, and sold it to *People* magazine for $3 million, which she donated to Patel's clinic. Patel was back helping children. Sam was still at StarView, helping addicts regain their lives they'd lost to drugs.

Sam had truly helped my mother. She was sober. Thoughtful, most of the time. More centered, maybe because for the first time in her life she was in love. Oh, and the scorpion bracelet was on her wrist again, glittering with every dramatic gesture.

As for me, I never called my agent back. Heath was taking me to the shooting range. He said I had natural ability. Soon I'd have my PI license. The blue Tiffany gun was framed behind glass. It was going to be the first thing I'd hang in my office. Once I found an office. I wanted it to remind me of my big lie. And of Tanya, who'd saved my life and my mother's. And in a way, Ryan's.

Now my mother saw me, got up from the sofa, and came out to join me on the deck, bringing her seductive energy with her.

"I'm sorry," she said.

"It's worked out."

"No. I mean truly, deeply sorry." Her frank blue eyes commanded mine.

My shoulders tensed.

"I betrayed you in the worst possible way, Diana. It wasn't Colin's fault. It was mine."

"I don't want to talk about it."

"Sam says we should."

"Someday. I'm glad to have you back. Let's leave it there."

She sighed and took my hand. "I'm glad you're becoming a professional detective."

I smiled. "Are you really?"

"In all the publicity they keep referring to you as an amateur sleuth. You've never been an amateur at anything. You're always a pro." She kissed me on the cheek and went back to sit with Ryan.

Heath passed her in the doorway, carrying a glass of red wine in one hand and a beer in the other.

He handed me the wine. "How is Ryan doing?"

"He misses Tanya. But he's better."

Heath tipped his beer and drank. "Have you thought about my offer?"

"It's very generous. But I can't join your agency."

"We work well together."

"I'm a loner. You know that."

"This isn't Philip Marlowe times, Diana. Let me do something for you. How about I give Rodriquez to you?"

I looked him. "He's yours to give?"

He grinned

"What does Rodriquez think?"

"He's constantly hinting at it. Driving me crazy."

"He and I would be tough competition for you."

He chuckled. "It's Hollywood. There's plenty of work to go around."

"How's Madison?"

"She left me. Said I was too quiet, didn't know how to communicate."

"I'm glad you can't communicate." I slid my arm around his waist. My beast.

And that's how my life changed. By walking out on my own movie when I should've stayed and watched it one more time. But I'm glad I didn't.

# ACKNOWLEDGMENTS

Kudos to Claiborne Hancock, publisher of Pegasus Crime, and a man of unending patience. Thank you.

Love to my daughter, Erica McKee, an avid reader of mysteries, for reading the first few chapters and saying, "I love this, mom. Keep going."

Always to Gayle Lynds for her friendship, support, and her sharp writer's eye.

And to my dogs, Dr. Watson and Satchmo, who forced me to exercise by getting me up from my desk to let them out and let them in. (Repeat this endlessly.) They kept me company by wagging their tails, snoring, scratching, barking, farting and demanding to be fed. My writer's life would feel empty without them.

And last, but not least, to Jane Heller, who blithely threw out an idea that sent me on a journey of death and resurrection.